AFTER
THE WAVE

T0158233

AFTER
THE WAVE

Tew Bunnag

RIVER
BOOKS

First published and distributed in 2015 by
River Books
396 Maharaj Road, Tatien, Bangkok 10200
Tel. 66 2 622-1900, 224-6686
Fax. 66 2 225-3861
E-mail: order@riverbooksbk.com
www.riverbooksbk.com

Editor: Narisa Chakrabongse
Production supervision: Paisarn Piemmettawat
Design: Ruetairat Nanta

ISBN 978 616 7339 59 7

Printed and bound in Thailand
by Bangkok Printing Co., Ltd.

CONTENTS

The photographs in this book were taken by children from different communities in the Phangnga region of the Andaman coast who were affected by the Tsunami.

In 2007 Insight Out, a joint project initiated by photographers and writers in the region guided these children and those in the Banda Acheh district of Sumatra during a series of workshops aimed at empowering them to express and integrate what had happened to them and their families through words and images. This resulted in a much acclaimed travelling exhibition of the work produced. (See www.insightoutproject.org)

The author, who was involved with the project at the beginning would like to thank these children, and the Insight Out team, in particular Mr. Masaru Goto and Khun Suthep Kritsanavarin for their work with the children and for allowing the photographs to be used.

INTRODUCTION

The media makes sure that even those of us fortunate enough not to find ourselves in a conflict zone are fed images of war on a daily basis; evidence of our continuing disunity, barbarism and failure to find solutions except through the use of force and violence. Inevitably as we read about the latest atrocities in a newspaper or watch the recent scenes of carnage on the screen from the safety of our homes we take sides. That is the point. Conflict feeds conflict. War keeps dividing us. With all our intelligence we seem not yet to have noticed that we inhabit the same globe floating in space. We continue to fight and kill each other with righteousness. But when something like the Tsunami happens we are momentarily stunned and transported into a dimension of shared humanity and given a brief glimpse of how it might be beyond our differences. When the wave vented its destruction on 26th December 2004 it did not discriminate between skin colour, religious creed, political ideology, economic status or any of those factors that normally divide us. In that sense a natural disaster of such massive proportions as the Tsunami is a leveller and a unifier. Loss and grief have no boundaries. If only we could remember that.

None of the countries in the region that was hit by the wave, with the possible exception of Bangladesh, was adequately prepared. In the aftermath of the Tsunami this became rightly one of the ongoing issues.

Common sense tells us that a proper warning system would have saved lives and will do so in the future. But as for preparedness on the psychological level I am not so sure. It is not merely a question of establishing the necessary technology. How can we be prepared for such a dramatic expression of nature's power unless we are constantly in touch with it? And we no longer think that it is important to have this contact. We now dominate nature to such an extent that we no longer feel part of it and we have lost the means to be connected because the lines have been severed in our rush to exploit the wealth of our environment.

The only people that I saw in the South of Thailand who were prepared at all, and who as a consequence lost fewer lives were the Moken sea gypsies, an aboriginal people who have lived along the Andaman coast for centuries. Through their shamans they have always communed with the sea. The Tsunami wave, which they call the Labu, has always been a part of their culture. The wave of December 26th destroyed their homes but it did not leave them with the spiritual confusion that other communities along the coast have suffered.

From a personal perspective the Tsunami brought up for me yet again the question of fate, chance and synchronicity that has fascinated me for most of my life. I had booked a bungalow for a family holiday on the part of the coast that was hit but at the last minute, because my eldest daughter was going through the final stages of an uncomfortable pregnancy we decided to stay nearer Bangkok that weekend. So I cancelled the reservation.

Within a week after the Tsunami the organization for which I work in Bangkok (the Human Development Foundation based in Klongtoey) was contacted by the Southern Aids network who were afraid that after the disaster the poorest would be the last people to receive assistance and that those infected with the Aids virus would be forgotten altogether. Because of our experience in the Bangkok slums they asked us to go down to help. Overnight we became involved with projects in the deep South beginning with Satun near the Malaysian border. Then gradually, as more local groups contacted us we moved up to Phuket island and eventually to Phangnga province which was the hardest hit by the wave. We were asked to go where government projects either had not reached or were insufficient for the task of rehabilitation. This entailed working with a wide range of communities; Muslims, Moken Sea Gypsies, New Thai, Chow Lay. We were finding funds for children, helping to repair of houses and schools, providing sanitation systems and water deposits, rebuilding boats, organizing local communities with their documentation, replanting trees, as well as fulfilling our original mission which was to help the HIV positive population to continue with their lives.

I did not know the Andaman coast very well before I worked there and I cannot say that my knowledge of it is that extensive now. What I learned was firsthand from the people I met there and with whom I collaborated. Much of it was an eye opener. As usual the political, social and economic background along the coast is defyingly complex, with many layers to sift through before a clear picture emerges. The Tsunami destroyed lives. At the same time it also revealed much that was hidden away before.

In the course of my trips down there I met with many who had survived the wave but lost their entire family and others who had witnessed terrifying things. The stories that I heard from these people were, on the whole more extraordinary than anything a fiction writer could ever dream up. I have not made use directly of these personal episodes that were entrusted to me. But they have inspired me and in this little collection I have tried to filter what was given to me into stories that touch on the various aspect that I feel reflect what happened in the event and in its aftermath. The Tsunami was a phenomenon that changed the lives of everyone in the affected region. It has left much sadness in its wake, as well as puzzlement, and problems which are still to be resolved. I have told these stories to honour those who were killed, those who will carry their grief with them for the rest of their lives, and those who carry on courageously in their efforts to continue.

October 2005

LEK AND MRS. MILLER

The sun was coming up over the trees on the hill behind. The first rays were catching the waves as they broke gently to shore. This was the fourth time that Lek had watched the tall foreign woman with the freckled skin and straw coloured hair make her way down through the poolside area which was still only half repaired and onto the empty beach. She walked northward for about thirty metres. Then she stopped, took off her sandals, placed her leather shoulder bag on the sand, sat down with her legs stretched out in front of her and leaned her back against a fallen palm tree. There she stayed, still as a rock looking out to sea.

The quiet ritual that he witnessed once again evoked an unfamiliar emotion in Lek; a sort of longing that was intensified by the fact that every morning at this point he would have to leave. It was the end of his night shift and he had to hurry home to the "Temporary Housing Estate" where he and his family were now staying and take his little sister to school. But it was Saturday; there was no school. He had time to spare. He was not tired and he wanted to see what the woman would do next.

Normally in the high tourist season Lek would have been ready to drop by now. The nights would be long with the guests sitting by the pool drinking till all hours. Some might arrive back dead drunk from an evening on the town. He would then have to help them up to their rooms. There would be sick to clean, or a dispute with a taxi driver to settle. Worst of all, as far as Lek was concerned, was if the night manager had gone off to take a nap leaving him with the task of dissuading a guest from bringing in a boy or girl picked up in some karaoke bar or club along the coast. This usually developed into an unpleasant scene which he was too young to cope with. Foreigners puzzled him.

"Learn English and understand how the "farangs"* think. That's the way to get on in the world," his father had told him more than once.

The family was proud that he had got the job at the resort. It was getting harder and harder for a small time fisherman to make ends meet. Lek was seventeen and they wanted him to have a future. Learning English was not difficult. Lek had a good ear and quickly put together the phrases he heard repeated and although he was not yet able to carry on a long conversation he could get by well enough. But as for understanding foreigners he had to admit that it was hard work. After two years of being around the farangs and serving them he still did not really have a clue what they were about. For instance, he wondered at the way that they could lie out all day long under the blazing sun covering themselves with creams and lotions that did not stop them from turning lobster red by the evening. Where was the pleasure in that? Then there was the amount

*Farang is the term Thais use to describe foreigners and things foreign.

that they could drink! He once watched a group of Finnish visitors get through three cases of Vodka in one sitting without much sign of merriment. He also noticed the behaviour of the family members to one another, with so little respect. And, of course he was amazed at all the money that they had. He saw people spending in a week what his father earned in five years. No. The farangs remained a mystery to him.

Mrs. Miller was different. He felt that he knew her, that they were somehow connected. He had learned her name from the receptionist who checked her in. "She's here till Saturday," the girl told him. "But why are you so interested? She's older than your mother. Do you think she's going to pick you up and take you back to London and keep you in style as her toy boy?"

She had said all this as a joke. Lek, both embarrassed and annoyed had fumbled for an adequate answer but found none. He did not tell her that he found Mrs. Miller to be different from the other farangs he had met there, that her composure and the sadness that enveloped her like a transparent veil stirred in him a mixture of curiosity and protectiveness.

From the first moment he saw her he had guessed why she was there at the resort. The other foreigners were volunteers working in a village up the coast. She was certainly not one of them. Nor was she a tourist. She did not have the air of someone on holiday. Besides, no tourists were coming there any more. The whole coastline was still a mess. It had to be that she was there because of the Tsunami.

After the wave struck many foreigners had arrived looking for their loved ones. Especially in those first weeks there was an intense, desperate bustle about the place as though, repelled by the horror of what had happened the visitors wanted to be in and out of there as soon as possible. Lek soon came to recognize the stunned look of despair and grief on their faces. Mrs. Miller wore the same expression. Lek saw it in the mirror as he put her suitcase down in her room the evening she arrived. But there was also a steady, direct, kindly look in her eyes as she handed him the tip that made him wonder: why now after so many months? Was she still searching?

Lek felt sure that Mrs. Miller did not leave the resort once in the week that she was there to go shopping or to visit Phuket. He wanted to ask the day staff what she did with her time after he left each morning. But already stung by the receptionist's remarks he did not dare to enquire.

That morning as he watched her he remembered that she was leaving that very day and this made him decide to approach her. It was not in his character to go up to a guest and strike up a conversation like some of his co-workers. This was their way of practising their English. They were not really curious. Lek was too shy to do this. He always let the guest make the first move and then he would respond. But with Mrs. Miller, without knowing exactly why, he felt such an urge to make contact, just once before she disappeared back into her world, that he did not restrain himself. He was already forming an excuse to approach her that would not make it seem improper. He did not mind what the others would think if they saw him. He only knew that he had to act before it was too late.

So that Saturday morning he walked down the steps from the balcony and past the pool area intending to follow her to where she was sitting on the beach. He could see that the builders had been lazy. There were stacks of masonry and planks all over the place as though they had no motivation to finish the job. When he stepped onto the beach he took off his socks and shoes. The sand was still cool from the dew. Mrs Miller's footprints were fresh. As he made his way towards her he suddenly thought that he had made the wrong decision and was about to turn back. But she had seen him. In panic he tried to recall the excuse that he had rehearsed. But she was already waving him over and when he was close she motioned for him to sit down next to her. Then she turned and gazed back to the sea whose surface was now dancing in the sunlight. The two of them sat in silence watching a fishing boat slowly crossing the horizon. The sky was cloudless. There was a gentle breeze that carried the smell of seaweed. The water was emerald green.

It was a full five minutes before she spoke, addressing the space in front of them as though she was conversing with it or praying to it in a slow, deliberate voice. Lek could only make out some of what she was saying. He heard the names "Kate" and "Robert" uttered several times, and the words "daughter"and "grandson". Then she paused for a moment, took up her shoulder bag and out of it pulled a silver picture frame which she handed to Lek. Now as she spoke again she kept pointing aggressively at the photograph in it and back to her chest and her voice was quivering with emotion. Lek only caught the word "Christmas", which sounded like an accusation. But he could not follow what she was trying to explain to him and he was already formulating a sentence in his mind to tell her that he recognized them, the ones in the picture, that he had served her daughter many times, that he had kicked a ball by the pool with her grandson, that he was there when their bodies were found. But before he could tell her any of this she said in a quieter voice:

"And you?"

Lek was tongue-tied. His English seemed to have vanished. What he wanted to say was that on the morning of the Tsunami his youngest brother, who was the same age as her grandson had run out to catch the fish that were stranded by the sea as it receded, that father had run out after him and that both had been caught by the wave. He wanted to tell her that the house where he was born had been completely destroyed. There was no trace of it left in the sand. And that they had no land deeds. So for two months they were in an army tent until one day an official came and told them that they were being moved and that his mother, who had been driven half mad by the deaths of her husband

Prinya Varak, 10 years old.

and young child had taken them all to the local temple to make merit and give thanks for having any shelter at all.

Lek said none of this. Instead all that came out of his mouth was:

"My father. My brother."

Mrs. Miller looked at him for a long while and then heaved a deep sigh. As she did so she reached over and put her hand gently on top of his. Lek did not draw away but turned his own hand over and held hers tightly. In that touch he understood something that he knew would be with him for the rest of his life.

Later that day Mrs Miller left for Phuket from where she was flying to Bangkok and then on to London. After paying the bill she asked the manager for an envelope into which she put the picture frame. Then she wrote Lek's name on it. When he arrived for his night shift that evening he saw that that they were all smiling as if they were sharing some private joke.

"We'll have to watch you from now on," said the manager with a wink as he handed Lek his package. "You're getting too popular with the farang ladies."

The teasing went on for another month. Lek was not offended. He knew that there was no malice to it. He hung the photograph on the wall in the temporary shelter and looked at it from time to time. It showed Mrs. Miller's daughter wearing a sweater and jeans. By her side was the boy in a swimming costume looking cold. They were standing on a grey pebble beach. Behind them a wave was breaking in a dark sea. He was glad to have the picture. He had none of his father or his brother, only the images stored in his mind.

He thought once of writing to Mrs. Miller. It was easy enough to get her address from the registry. But in the end he decided that there was no point. They had met in a place beyond boundaries, a place opened up by the wave. That was enough.

A SIMPLE MISTAKE

Nai Chang took a long drag on his cigarette and blew the smoke towards the ceiling. He heard a sound over in the corner. Perhaps it was a rat scuttling about. Out of habit he propped himself up to have a better look and in that moment he felt the pain shoot through his left side, so strong that it took the wind out of him and nearly made him drop his cigarette. He wanted to shout out and curse but he knew that if he did so he would wake up the others, his wife next to him in the bed and the two children on the floor. He sank back onto the pillow, his brow covered in a cold sweat. After a few minutes the pain eased.

It was nearly dawn. The grey light was already entering the room. Somewhere in the distance a cock was crowing. He had to be up early to catch the morning crowd at the market. There was no more time to waste. He needed to get some rest. Reaching his hand down and finding the tin ashtray he stubbed out the cigarette in one rough movement. Then, settling back he willed himself to stop thinking and to go to sleep. He had been doing this through the night without success and soon, to his frustration Nai Chang found himself once more going over the events that had taken place over the past month trying to see yet again if, as his wife said, they could really have been avoided.

The previous evening he had been sitting with two friends, both drivers like himself, at Mae Khem's noodle stall on the beach near Ta Chatchai. Before the wave the whole area was full of such places but now hers was the only one that had reopened. It had been another long day with little to show for it. The air was unseasonably heavy and close and they were complaining yet again of the lack of tourists. Mae Khem had just served them a bottle of ice cold beer which was helping to restore their good humour.

"If the farangs don't come back we'll all end up catching crabs to sell," said one of them and they all laughed because it was the last thing any of them wanted to do.

They had finished ordering some food when a white pickup truck roared up. Out of it jumped three young men who were muscular and fit and dressed in jeans, tee shirts and colourful trainers. One of them wore a blue baseball cap. They walked quickly to where Nai Chang and his companions were sitting and without so much as a greeting pulled him out of his seat and pummelled him with kicks and punches. The others sat and watched without helping. Afterwards they apologized but there was no need. Nai Chang knew how scared they were and how fear can paralyze you. In their position he would have done the same. The young men were professionals who were good at their job. They could have killed him if they had wanted to but when they had hurt him enough the one with the baseball cap stopped them and, bending down to Nai Chang said:

"No more talk of ghosts, OK? Next time we'll take your seelaw* apart."

They left him groaning in the sand. His friends wanted to take him directly to the hospital but he would not let them. After a while he was able to sit up.

"I've been beaten up worse than that in my life," he told them, and it was true."No real harm done."

This last remark was more to reassure himself. When they had finished their beers the two companions helped him home. When his wife saw the state he was in she cried and said that she knew that it would happen, and to his annoyance the others agreed with her. And secretly so did he. There was no doubt in any of their minds what the beating was about. The young thug's mention of the ghosts had said it all.

How could it have been avoided? After all he was only doing his job driving around looking for a fare, and there they were standing on a deserted corner near Kamala beach. It was nearly evening and the light was fading. He was hungry and wanted to get home. But what could he do? He had hardly covered the cost of the petrol that day. Business was bad as usual. Only the seelaws parked on the sea front at Patong were making a decent living. The rest of them were struggling. The

*a seelaw is a motorized four wheeler used as a taxi.

tourists were beginning to trickle back but there were nowhere near the numbers like before. Anyway, when he saw the couple Nai Chang instinctively slowed down in case they wanted a ride and sure enough as he drew closer they were waving at him. It was a foreign couple, backpacker types. The man was tall and had a Rasta hairstyle, wore a sleeveless tee shirt, kaki shorts and flip flops. The girl had on a skimpy top and a long skirt. Both were blonde and carried identical shoulder bags embroidered with Northern tribal designs. These details were to prove important later on.

The man spoke to him in English and told him that they wanted to go to Phuket town. They agreed on a price. It meant turning round and going back the way that he had just come and half way across the island. But Nai Chang did not mind. They climbed in and he started the motor. The couple did not speak to each other once during the whole journey. Every time he looked in the mirror he saw them both looking out to either side. It occurred to him that they might have had an argument. The girl's long hair blew in the breeze. He noticed nothing else in particular.

About two kilometres away from the main town they came up to a small market by the roadside. The man suddenly tapped Nai Chang's shoulder and motioned for him to stop ahead at a siding where motorbikes were parked with their riders sitting astride them talking. In itself there was nothing strange in this request. Nai Chang presumed that the farangs wanted to buy something in the market, a bottle of water or perhaps some fruit. They both climbed out and he glanced round to see them approaching a stall at the entrance. He took the opportunity to light up a cigarette. After a few minutes he looked round again. But now they were nowhere to be seen. He got out and walked over to the stall where they had been.

"Auntie,"he said to the old lady running it. "Where did those farangs go?"

"What are you talking about? I didn't see any farangs," she replied brusquely.

Thinking that she might have had a problem with her memory Nai Chang merely shrugged, left her and strolled into the market thinking that he would find them there. The lights had already come on inside. Each stall was brightly lit up. Most of them sold dried fish products and bottled sauces and the strong local shrimp paste whose smell hung heavily in the air. It was not a tourist market. There were very few customers about and no sign of the couple. Outside it was now dark. Nai Chang was puzzled. There were no buildings in the vicinity and behind the market there was a steep and thickly wooded hill where no one lived. He could not understand where they had gone. Of course it crossed his mind that they had cheated him. But for so little! And besides, why, if they were going to go off without paying, would they have chosen that out of the way market instead of somewhere a little nearer to their destination?

He walked over to the bikers.

"Did you see where those farangs went?" he asked them.

"There were no farangs in your seelaw. You came alone, uncle," one of them replied.

Nai Chang looked long and hard at the young man who had just spoken. He had been driving for thirty years. He had dealt with many people. He could tell if they were lying or not. The young man looked straight back at him. "Honestly, uncle. We've been sitting here all the time and we've seen no farangs."

"In that case they must have been ghosts," said Nai Chang.

When he got home that evening he told his wife, Mali about the incident and the next morning she insisted on going to a temple where they asked a monk to say prayers and sprinkle blessed water over the seelaw to rid it of bad spirits and to protect Nai Chang from any further encounters.

That would have been the end of the story if Nai Chang had listened to his wife, a superstitious woman when she told him never to mention the incident to anybody because it was bad luck to have seen ghosts and even worse to have the reputation of being able to see them. But about a week later Nai Chang found himself parked outside a café in the Patong district which had been popular with the tourists before the wave hit. This had been one of his regular patches where he never had to wait very long before a farang came up to hire him to go round the island sightseeing or to a beach on the other side. But since the Tsunami he had not been back for some time. He happened to be there that morning because he had just dropped off a woman at a market nearby and he thought it was a good moment to have a rest and a smoke. As he lit up he noticed a large poster that had been stuck onto the wall outside the café. There had been many of these in the first months after the wave and people would crowd round to see if they could recognize any of the photographs of those who were still missing. There was always a contact number, and sometimes a reward was offered. Nowadays there were few of these posters left round the island and Nai Chang did not even bother to look at them properly since he knew that those who had not been found by now must be dead. But that morning two images made him get out of his seelaw and take a closer look. They were next to one another in the top left hand corner. Nai Chang squinted and thrust his face nearer and nearer to the poster and then suddenly, addressing no one in particular and practically jumping in the air with excitement he exclaimed:

"But it's them! I picked them up the other day."

A voice from behind him said:

"Are you sure?"

This took him completely by surprise. He turned round to face a young woman in dark glasses smiling at him pleasantly.

"Yes," said Nai Chang after a moment's hesitation. He looked back at the photographs, the Rasta hairstyle, the blonde hair. Who else could it have been?

"And where did you pick them up?"

"Over near Kamala beach," he replied.

"And when was this exactly?"

Nai Chang was beginning to find it strange that this woman was questioning him in such a direct manner. At the back of his mind he remembered what his wife had told him. The woman, sensing his dilemma said:

"I'm sorry for asking you these things. I don't mean to be rude. I'm a journalist from the Bangkok News and they've sent me down here to do a piece on Phuket. I just find your story so fascinating. I'd love to hear more. Can I offer you lunch?"

Nai Chang was disarmed by her politeness, but he still resisted. Smiling at her he shifted from one foot to the other. The woman added, casually:

"Of course I will pay for your time. It's only fair."

She seemed friendly and sincere so Nai Chang let himself be persuaded. They went to a nearby restaurant, a simple place near the beach. The woman ordered a beer for him. Then when the food arrived she took out a small recorder and switched it on. "So, please tell me everything that happened."

Nai Chang took his time and described the whole incident as faithfully as he could. The woman seemed very pleased. Before she left she took several pictures of him standing next to his seelaw. Then she thanked him and handed him a generous amount as they said goodbye. At first he would not take the money.

"But you agreed. Please. What you've told me today will really give the article an edge."

So in the end he was persuaded to accept.

She had told him that the piece was due to come out that weekend and sure enough the following Sunday morning Nai Chang was woken up early by the sound of a motorbike outside his front door. It was Ai Kao, his young cousin who worked in the airport and who had brought the first edition of Bangkok News with him.

"Pi Chang, you're famous. Look! It's on page four. Why didn't you tell me? See. There's your picture too."

Nai Chang could scarcely believe his eyes. He had never imagined that he would ever see his photograph in a newspaper. Next to it was a caption that read:

"Phuket. Ghost island?"

Nai Chang, who had not finished school, read slowly, mouthing some of the words out loud. The article consisted of stories that the journalist had accumulated about the strange incidents that had allegedly taken place on the island since the Tsunami. For instance, there was a shopkeeper who claimed to have seen an elderly foreigner walk out of her store and evaporate into thin air, a hotel worker who heard a young woman crying in a room that was empty, a fisherman who in broad daylight watched a child walking on the waves, and many others. His own story was the centrepiece and she not only reproduced it word for word as he had recounted it to her, but also complimented him for the clarity of his description.

When he had finished reading he noticed that Mali was standing at his shoulder. For a moment he thought that she would be cross. But she was smiling as she shook her head.

"Well, well. You are famous."

He knew from the way she spoke that despite what she had said before she was proud of him.

Fame meant that Nai Chang was now recognized all over the island. For a man who had grown up in poverty and who was aware of his lowly position on the social scale this was intoxicating and all the more so for having come out of the blue. Wherever he went strangers would now come up and clap him on the back and tell him that they had seen the article. He became a kind of folk hero. People would hire him to take them home just to have a chat and share their own stories with him. Some even bought him a meal and a drink for the chance to hear him repeat his tale, which little by little he learned to embellish in order to please his audience.

It was like a dream and for a while Nai Chang, who had never known such attention, basked in the glory. Whatever doubt or apprehension he had about the whole situation he kept to himself. Only when he lay in bed at night after a day's work would he sometimes think that perhaps he might have been mistaken, perhaps in the half light he had not really seen the couple in the poster but other farangs who looked like them. This thought would produce a moment of anxiety but then he would dismiss it by telling himself that they had to be the same ones. And besides, it was too late to change the way things were going. For whatever else his fame meant neither he nor Mali could complain because they both saw that his income had increased considerably as a consequence of the article.

Events took a strange turn one morning when he woke up to find a television crew on his front porch. They had given him no warning that they were coming and had obtained his address from another seelaw driver. Their team leader, a young man who was far less polite than the female journalist he had met previously told him that they were making a documentary on Phuket and on the aftermath of the wave, that they had read the piece in the Bangkok news, and that they now wanted to film him and take him to the place where he had picked up the farang couple and follow the route to the market where he had last seen them. Again, when he heard the proposal Nai Chang hesitated. This was going too far, he thought, and he did not like these television people very much. But they were there on his doorstep. How could he refuse? So once more he allowed himself to be persuaded, this time with the help of an even bigger sum to cover his expenses and the day's shooting.

The program was watched all over Thailand. In the little cluster of buildings where Nai Chang lived, just off the highway near the bridge to the mainland it was an excuse for a party. Three television sets were placed on chairs by the road outside the corner shop so that everyone could have a good view. Friends came in from neighbouring villages. Seelaws, motorbikes, pickups were parked all over the place. Everyone brought food and drink. There was fish grilled on earthen stoves and plenty of beer and whiskey. Two hours before the show came on most of the adults were getting high and singing to a karaoke machine. Then when it was time to watch the program Ai Kao, who was already drunk shouted for everybody to be quiet.

Nai Chang came across well. He spoke quietly and with a lucidity that comes with familiarity. After all he had had plenty of time to rehearse the story. And he managed to control himself and not overdo the telling so that everything he said sounded plausible and convincing. The interviewer pressurized him several times about what had actually taken place. But Nai Chang was up to the questions and sharp with his answers and provided such a wealth of information and detail that it seemed impossible that he could have made up such a story.

As soon as it was over there was a loud cheer from all those present led by Ai Kao. Then one by one they all came up to congratulate Nai Chang who, sitting on a white plastic chair nursing a glass of whiskey and too far gone to be able to move accepted their praises like some superstar. At around eleven most people had left. Nai Chang himself wanted to stagger back to his house and sleep. But there was a small group of people left who were still drinking. By this time Ai Kao was hardly making sense but he continued to pour out the drinks and insisting that the party carry on till dawn. "It's not often something like this happens," he said in a slurred voice to whoever was listening. "We should all be proud of Pi Chang."

With that he raised his glass yet again and the others did the same.

"But there's one thing I don't understand. Those bastards. What were they going on about?"

What Ai Kao was referring to was an interview towards the end of the program. Some local businessmen were being filmed having lunch in a restaurant and asked what they thought of the ghost stories that were circulating.

"It can only be bad news for us," one said.

"They're lying," said another. " But it's too late. The damage has already been done. The Chinese won't come back now. They're afraid of ghosts."

"But there's little we can do about it," added a third.

Apparently the others had paid little attention to that part of the program. But Nai Chang, even in his drunkenness had made a mental note of it because he had an instant premonition of what was to happen.

There was no way that he was going to get any sleep now. The children were already stirring. In less than an hour they would be fully awake and up and about getting ready for school. Nai Chang, avoiding any abrupt movement because of his pain, carefully rolled his body over so that it was now facing his wife. She was still deep in sleep, her head resting in the crook of her arm. For a while in the dim light he studied her soft, flat features and listened to her steady breathing.

He wished he had listened to her at the very beginning. But it was too late. Still, on reflection he had to admit that he had learned a valuable lesson; namely that fame came with a price. It was something that nobody could teach you. You had to learn it for yourself, and for that he was grateful. But what made him bitter was that he had not asked for any of it in the first place. It was not as if he had gone out looking to tell his tale to anybody. Fate had brought the journalist to him. Then again he knew that if he had kept his wits about him he could always have said no to her. So in the end he had to accept that it was a lesson of Karma and Vibhakka; action and its consequences. Having once been a temple boy he had heard the monks preaching this so many times that he knew it by heart. But only now did he understand exactly what it meant.

The episode was not quite over. The question still remained: what was he to do if someone else were to come up and ask him about the ghosts he had seen? How could he now back down from the story that he had told to the whole world? And yet if he did not deny it he was sure that the hoodlums would be true to their word. Someone had given them their orders. And if they came back to wreck his vehicle it would be a total disaster. He was a seelaw driver. He could not think of doing anything else.

In the end he saw that the only way out of the whole mess was to swallow his pride and, if asked again about the incident, to say that he had made a simple mistake, that the farangs he had picked up were not the same as the ones in the photograph, that they had not vanished, that he had dropped them off at their destination. If it took this lie for him to be left in peace and to carry on earning his living, then it was fine by him. What choice did a poor man like him have?

Nai Chang's bruises took about two weeks to heal properly. Word spread fast all over the island that he had been beaten up. It was obvious just from seeing his battered face. And everyone knew why. No one pestered him any more to repeat his ghost story. It was as if they avoided him in case his bad luck rubbed off on them. Nai Chang did not mind. He wanted to be left alone and to recover his former anonymity. The only thing that he regretted was that his income was now back to where it was. Like the other drivers he would have to ride out the season and pray that the tourists would come back one day like before. In the meantime he would have to be content with picking up the occasional ghost.

Prasit Kiewnil, 11 years old.

Samnieng's Mixed Blessing

Sunday was not normally her rest day but Samnieng had no strength to go to work. She sat on the edge of the bed looking at the alarm clock and seeing, with regret that it was far too late for her to make it up to the main road and catch the company bus. She had sweated so much during the night that the mattress was still soaked. Her head was throbbing and her chest was so tight that she could hardly get any air into her lungs. But she knew that she could not stay lying down. She had to focus herself and muster up the energy to get the food cooked for her three daughters and see them bathed and dressed. This should already have been done much earlier. There was no school, of course, because it was Sunday but it had been arranged that her friend Chalaw was coming round to pick them up after they had eaten and take them to her house in the next village where she was going to look after them until Samnieng came home from work.

On any other day her mother would have helped. But her parents were away visiting her brother and his family down the coast in Krabi and would not be home till the middle of the week. There was no one to rely on, not even the neighbours since the row between them and her father the week before; a stupid argument over local politics fuelled by too much cheap whiskey. So she had no choice that morning but to cook the rice herself and get the girls off before she could collapse.

As she sat there in her old, faded sarong Samnieng looked out of the back window as she always did before getting bathed and dressed. That morning the sea was grey green, its surface strangely cloudy. In the distance Samnieng could see two fishing boats returning from their night's catch. They were too far away for her to know for sure but she guessed that they were from the sea gypsy village up the coast.

She liked the light at this hour. It was still soft and dreamy unlike the harsh sunlight later in the day. The sand looked so white that it was luminous. She had been looking out through this window as long as she could remember and yet she was still thrilled by the beauty of what she saw. There was the scent of the early morning air; frangipani mixed with the salt and the seaweed. She had only been away twice from the house in all of her 25 years, once to her brother's wedding and another time to stay with her husband in hospital while he lay dying. Both times she missed the sea and particularly the sight through the back window, which nothing could replace. Her father often said that although they were poor they lived in the best spot in the whole world, right there on the beach where his own father, a fisherman had moved the family just before he died.

" The farangs pay good money to come here year after year. But we're poor and we're here all the time," he would say, laughing and she would understand exactly why he found it funny.

Samnieng stood up unsteadily and walked over to where her three daughters were sleeping and with one hand propped against the wall she bent down to watch them for a while. They were all huddled together in a ball, their arms and legs intertwined so that they looked like one body. This made her smile. She noticed that the bed was getting too small for them. Soon they would have to put the mattress on the floor. She did not want to do this because sometimes a rat made its way into the room and the thought that it would walk over her children repelled her. Worse still was if a snake should slither in while they were sleeping. But what could she do? A new bed was expensive.

Of the three girls only the youngest, Jum who was four years old, looked like her. The other two, Noi and Ann took after their father, with his fine features, curly hair and dark skin. Manit, her late husband, was from the other side of the island facing the mainland. He was older than her, had done time in jail for dealing drugs and had a reputation as a lady's man. They met at her brother's wedding party in Krabi when Samnieng was just sixteen. He had flirted with her and seduced her the next day. Ten months later, having left school she gave birth to Noi. Then eighteen months after that came Ann. When the first two were born she and Manit were doing well together. He was driving a truck up and down the coast delivering sand and cement for a local firm and providing enough for the family. He had been through a rough patch but it looked like he was finding his feet again. Samnieng's parents liked him. He was a good storyteller and Samnieng's father enjoyed drinking with him.

One day a friend of Manit persuaded him to quit the job and drive a taxi instead. There was a lot of work on the coast. Tourism was booming and there were not enough taxi drivers. Manit, a restless type was ready for change. He told Samnieng that it would mean that he could spend more time with her and the babies. But it was not true; in fact, precisely the opposite. There seemed to be work to do day and night, especially in the high season when he would sometimes be hired to go long distances, up towards Ranong, down to Satun on the border, or to the other coast as far North as Chumpon. By the time Jum was born Samnieng knew that if things did not change then she was practically alone as a single mother.

During the next couple of years Manit spent more and more time away and Samnieng noticed that whenever he came back home he was drinking heavily. Whenever she asked him where he had been he would make an angry face, swear, and raise his hand as if to hit her. He never did, but the gesture alone was violent enough to stop her questioning him any further. Then one day he got blind drunk and told her that he was ill, that he had Aids and that she should have a check up too. She could not believe what she was hearing. What had he done? Where did he catch it? He would not tell her immediately. It was much later when he was really sick that he confessed to her how he had been going to a karaoke bar in Takua Pa with a friend and how they went with the girls there, and how they were both infected.

Samnieng went to the local hospital and had her blood tested. When the results came back they told her that she was HIV positive. Even though Manit insisted that he had contracted the disease after Jum was born the doctor arranged for her to get her daughters tested just to be safe. It turned out that they were all in the clear. But even though this was good news it did not make Samnieng happy to think that if both Manit and she died the children would be left on their own. She had seen this happen to some families in the villages nearby and she was frightened for them. When the parents were gone the little ones left behind were always vulnerable and it was up to the angels what became of them. The only comforting thought was that her parents were good people who would not abandon her or her girls. She was certain of this when she finally found the courage to tell them that she had been infected. They had both cried and promised her that they would stand by her. The doctor also tried to reassure her and told her not to worry, that her count was relatively low and that she had every chance of carrying on with a normal life as long as she did what she was told.

Meanwhile she watched Manit go downhill rapidly. After finding out about his condition he seemed to give up altogether. He drank even more and became depressed to such a point that he did not bother to take the pills that he had been prescribed. His body soon became covered with sores and rashes and he began to lose weight at an alarming rate. The three little girls watched all of this not understanding why their father was fading away before their very eyes. Then one day Samnieng could not look after him in the house any more. She took him to Phuket where he was admitted to the public hospital and she spent three nights sleeping on a bench in the corridor until he died.

That had all happened a year earlier when the youngest was still three. Samnieng had no one now but her parents. But kind and generous as they were they did not have the means to look after her family. School meals, uniforms, exercise books, pencils, not to mention the food all cost money that they did not have. Her father worked as a carpenter in a small boatyard. There was no way that he could make enough to keep all of them. So in the end Samnieng, who had no training in any skills decided to take whatever job she could find. It was her friend Chalaw who told her that a construction company nearby was looking for labourers. There was an extension to a resort up the coast near Tung Wa being built and they were offering 185 baht per day including free transport from the pick up point and a midday meal. It seemed fair. Samnieng had always been fit and strong having grown up by the sea with the good clean air and fresh food. At that stage the virus did not seem to have made a difference to her health. Even so she found the job tiring at first because she was not used to labouring and her body ached from the lifting and the carrying that she had to do all day long. But she soon got used to it and after a while it did not require much effort.

In fact things were fine until that morning, which was why she was so downhearted. She could not understand how she could be feeling so ill. She had been taking her medicine everyday on time. She did not smoke or drink unlike her friend Chalaw and, of course she had not had sex. She did not indulge in self pity, thinking too much about the past. Despite everything that had happened with Manit she had kept positive and managed to stave off all the demons in her mind. This was very important, they had told her at the clinic, and she had followed their advice. In a word, she had done everything right. Nevertheless, she had failed.

Missing the day's work was a big problem. She was already thinking of the excuse that she would give to the foreman the next day, presuming that she was well enough to go and see him. She would say that she had a bad dose of 'flu'. The only trouble was that he was no fool. She was sure that when he saw the state she was in he would immediately guess what the problem was. She knew that she had to be ready to be fired. They had no need to keep her on. There was plenty of work on the island and people were arriving every day from other provinces. There was building going on everywhere. As a cheap labourer they hired you on the spot and gave you a hat and a uniform. Most of all she did not want the foreman, a decent man who she respected, to know the real cause of her absence. No one in the community knew for certain that she was infected except her parents and she wanted to keep it that way.

Samnieng went into the small kitchen at the side of the house next to the toilet. She took some rice out of the jar in the corner, filled a saucepan of water from the tap and lit the gas stove. There was some fish left over from the previous evening's meal. It was enough for now. Chalaw would feed them later on. Samnieng sat down on the floor, wiped the sweat from her face and touched her forehead with the back of her hand. She was still feverish.

As she waited for the rice to cook she started to think ahead. If she were to lose the job she would offer to help Chalaw's mother who had just been given the money by her daughter to buy a washing machine so that she could take in laundry from the villagers and earn herself some extra cash. Samnieng was sure that the old lady would need someone to help her with the ironing. It would mean less pay than the construction site but it would also be less tiring and she would be nearer home. She would talk to Chalaw about it when she came to fetch the children. Chalaw had always been her best friend. They had grown up together and gone to the same school up the road where all the children from the villages in that area went. When Samnieng got pregnant it was Chalaw who encouraged her to keep the baby.

"Don't get rid of it. That wouldn't be right," she had said at the time." I will help you look after your child."

Looking back Samnieng thought that they were both naïve to think that having a baby was like playing with dolls. But when Noi was born she was glad that she had taken Chalaw's advice even though her friend was not around to help her as she had promised. For Chalaw herself had left school soon after Samnieng and disappeared to Bangkok for a few years. By the time she came back from the capitol they all saw that she had changed. Her innocence had gone. Chalaw never liked to talk about this period but it was obvious that in Bangkok she had learned about clothes and makeup and men. On her return she quickly found work in a massage parlour in Phuket and started earning more than anyone else in the village. Nobody looked down on her. The general opinion was that if she could manage to earn that much money then good luck to her. And why go all the way to Bangkok to ply your trade when there was plenty of work in your own back yard? As for Samnieng, she was only too happy to see that her old friend was back. She did not judge her for earning a livelihood in that way because she knew that if circumstances were different she too might have done the same.

Soon after the rice was cooked the girls were up. They came trouping into the kitchen and when they saw their mother there they looked surprised.

"Aren't you going to go to work today, Mae?" asked Ann. "You told us you'd leave the food and see us when you got back. You're not even dressed yet. You've missed the bus."

"I don't have to be there till later today," said Samnieng.

"It's OK. I'll go when you're gone. I'll tidy up round here first." She tried to sound as convincing as she could but she knew that the older ones understood that she was unwell. She who had always been strong and healthy and busy about the house could hardly move that morning and she saw that they noticed this.

All three children went out the back to bathe and to put on their clothes with unusual quietness. It was nearly nine o'clock, which was when Chalaw was coming round for them. She was usually late but they did not mind because it was worth the wait. She bought them sweets and ice creams during the day whenever she took them back and if they were lucky she would even take them for a ride in her brother's seelaw. They loved her for her kindness and generosity.

While she watched her daughters eating their breakfast Samnieng was praying her friend to be on time just for this once. She was feeling so weak that she could not last out a moment longer. She wanted her daughters to be out of there so that she could crash down on her bed. But she sensed that they were worried and, to reassure them she said, trying to sound cheerful.

"Look, I'm going to get dressed right now and maybe I'll go along with you to Auntie Chalaw's on my way to work."

Samnieng went out of the back door onto the little patio facing the beach where they bathed, washed the clothes, and cleaned the vegetables. She sat down for a moment on a low wooden stool to gather her strength. Her uniform was hanging on a hook on the wall but she did not know if she had enough energy left to put it on. She looked to the sea as though searching for the momentum that she needed.

At that precise second she saw something that she had never seen in her life. The water started to recede, not steadily as when a wave pulls back before curling in again but as though a plug had suddenly been pulled and the water was rushing away towards the horizon in quick time. She could see the fish floundering and jumping in the air all over the wet, ribbed sand, and the crabs scurrying around crazily. Old anchors were sticking up off the seabed together with bottles and everything else thrown out of the boats since time began. She might have walked out if she had been well because the fish were there for the taking. With a bucket she could have collected enough to sell to the neighbours in the next village and keep some for a good evening meal. But in the condition she was in she could only sit there and watch, fascinated and awestruck. Then from the back of her mind she recalled a word that she had heard when she was young, a Moken sea gypsy word that a little boy's mother had once uttered when she was telling her child off and threatening him with punishment. Labu. The Giant Wave.

"The Labu is going to come and gobble you up if you go on doing that," the mother had said.

Samnieng connected the spectacle that she was witnessing with that word, Labu and suddenly she forgot her tiredness and the fever and the pain in her chest. She tore the sarong off, pulled on a pair of trousers and a tee shirt. At the same time she was shouting out to the children:

"Girls, we've got to run! Right now!"

Long after the wave had gone Samnieng remembers it as a sea monster rearing its white head and roaring and she can hear the sound as it tore inland, crushing the trees and houses in its wake.

That Sunday morning she carried the youngest, Jum in her arms. The others were ahead of her as they ran and ran in mad desperation till they eventually reached a piece of high ground where other people had gone. Then they turned to look.

The first months were rough. After the wave they ended up in a temple sala* for a week among the wounded and the homeless. A wooden warehouse in the grounds

*sala is a hall in a temple.

Narumon Wongsit, 12 years old.

had been turned into a makeshift morgue. The stench of death in the air was overpowering. Then they were moved to an encampment set up by the army. It was there that her parents, returning from Krabi had found her and her children. Naturally they were all pleased to be reunited but now they were without a home and Samnieng was very sick by this time. Only her determination to keep her children afloat was keeping her going; that and the prayers that she offered up to the angels.

One morning a local official came to their tent and told them that they were to be moved again, this time to a temporary housing estate up the coast. So they all climbed onto an army truck along with the other "lucky ones" and were taken forty kilometres north and then up a winding dirt road to a place that had just been built in a clearing on the hillside. It housed about 300 people in all including some Muslim and sea gypsy families. The buildings had been hastily constructed and were hardly comfortable or homely; hardboard floor and walls, a corrugated iron roof, a water tap at the end of each row of dwellings. There was dust everywhere because the dry season was just beginning. But it was definitely better than the army camp they had left. So they gave thanks and lit candles and incense and counted their blessings.

By now Samnieng's health had deteriorated seriously. Even at the army camp she could barely lift herself off the bed. Now with the move the life force seemed to be seeping away from her altogether. She had lost a lot of weight because she could hardly eat or digest her food and as soon as they arrived at the temporary housing estate she collapsed on a mattress on the floor of her shelter unable to help with any of the tasks at hand. By this time she had no medicine left and in her heart she secretly thought she was soon going to end up like her husband. But a nurse who was visiting the community examined her on the second day and, seeing her condition arranged for her to be immediately transported to Phuket and admitted to the main hospital where she remained for over two weeks on saline drips. There were nights when she felt so sick that she wished that the wave had taken her and finished her off. But then she thought of the children and she willed herself to stay alive for them until they could fend for themselves. And eventually, little by little, she recovered her strength.

While she was away there was a constant flow of activity in the housing estate as more people arrived to set up their new living quarters. There were groups of Thais and foreigners working for various NGO's who came in to visit every day bringing food and plenty of clothing which came in huge crates on the back of trucks that travelled down from Bangkok. Teams of doctors and nurses and social workers were also busy checking the people staying there. Details were taken down over and over again about the livelihood that they had before the Tsunami and the property they owned and whether or not they held the land deeds to those properties or whether they were squatters. The general atmosphere was one of chaos and uncertainty. The wave had washed away the solid ground of all their lives.

When Samnieng left the hospital and returned to the housing estate she saw that things had changed. In the short time she had been gone a new communal kitchen and eating area had been constructed and there was now a playschool that had been paid for and set up by a foreign NGO whose volunteers were living among them in the estate and helping to look after the children. Samnieng's three girls, like all the other children who had survived, were still in deep shock and found it difficult to adapt to the new environment. While Samnieng was in hospital they had been looked after by the grandparents and when she arrived back they all rushed up to her and burst out crying uncontrollably as though all the tension that had accumulated during that past month could now be released. Samnieng did not know what she could do for them. But as the weeks went by she could see that they were beginning to feel more at home in the housing estate. Jum was still clinging to her but the other two were starting to make friends. Noi played all day with a little girl called Gop who had lost her father, a fisherman, and her brother to the wave.

Gop's older brother, Lek was one of the very few in the whole estate who still had employment. He worked in a resort nearby. Parts of it had been severely damaged but the main building was intact and had been turned into a centre for coordinating the foreign volunteers in that area. Lek normally worked night shift. Before going off he would play with his sister and help out with the other children. Samnieng envied him for having a job. She was stronger now and wanted to work again. The government had given her 30,000 baht as compensation for which she was suitably grateful but she knew that it would be used up in no time at all. And then what were they to do, with no longer a home to go to? She wanted to be earning a living so that she could put something aside for the future, for her children.

But the trouble was that there were no jobs to be had. During the reconstruction program organized by the government young soldiers were being brought into the area to build new dwellings for those who had lost their homes. They were only employing skilled locals to help them. There was no other construction work during those first because no one knew what the future was going to be for businesses on that coast.

Samnieng was frustrated by the situation but there was nothing that she could so she decided that instead of sitting watching television all day in the café she would spend her time helping to look after the children in the playschool and helping out in the communal kitchen. It was in this way that she started to get to know Lek who was also helping in the playschool from time to time. She noticed him from the very beginning because he seemed so friendly to everyone. She learned that his family, who were local people, had lost everything that they owned. It took a couple of months before they became real friends. But when they finally started talking and discussing all the things that had happened to them and to their families and all the episodes and intrigues that were going on in the estate they found that they shared the same way of looking at things and the same sense of humour.

One day Samnieng summoned up the courage to tell Lek that she was HIV positive. He told her that he had already heard. She asked if he minded.

" No. Why should I? I'm sorry you were infected. That's all," was his reply.

By now they had been there for almost a year. The dry season had given way to the rains and now the cooler weather was coming. About half of the original crowd who had arrived at the beginning had already moved on. Some of them went back to their villages when their houses had been repaired. Others were waiting to occupy the new buildings that the government put up. The Sea Gypsies looked as though they were going to be there for a long time because their land had been appropriated, as they had no papers to prove ownership. The authorities had offered them another piece of property to set up their village but they had collectively refused arguing that they had been living on the same patch of beach ever since any of them could remember and saw no reason why anyone had the right to claim it.

As far as Samnieng and her family were concerned they were stuck in another legal no man's land. They had a house registration but no title deeds to the land because her grandfather had squatted it. This was a common impasse and one that the government vowed would be resolved in time. But there seemed to be no solution in the short term and not much effort on the part of the officials to find one because they were too busy trying to revive local businesses to get involved in the issue. So they just had to wait and see what was going to happen. Lek's family faced the same problem.

On one of his days off Lek invited Samnieng and her girls to have a meal with him so that Noi and his sister Gop could play together. Both were in the same class and getting along well. That morning Lek's mother got some fresh crabs and a fish to curry. Samnieng and her daughters arrived in their best clothes. The donors in Bangkok were generous. There were plenty of dresses and tops to choose from. It was the first time that Samnieng and her girls had an occasion to wear them and to visit anyone.

She was curious to see where he lived, which turned out to be a room next to where his mother and sister slept. From the outside it was like all the others but inside she saw that he had turned it into his very own space. A moped was parked in the far corner and his clothes were hanging up neatly on a line that had been strung across one side of the room. She noticed that above his bed there was a photograph in a silver picture frame. " Who's that foreign woman? And is that her son?" she asked straightaway.

"Yes," he said." They died in the Tsunami."

"Did you know them well?"

"No. Not really. But I met the woman's mother. She gave me the photo."

Samnieng did not ask any more about the people in the picture. There were so many stories that she had heard. She was sure that Lek would tell her more when the time was right.

After the meal Lek and Samnieng decided to take a walk down the dirt track and head towards the sea. The excuse was that there was something that Lek wanted to buy from the 7/11 store in the village on the main road. The girls stayed at home with Lek's mother to look after them.

The afternoon was drowsy with heat. They walked slowly and in silence. Everyone was staying indoors with their fans turned on high. The estate, empty of people and with many of the rooms now abandoned and locked up looked particularly desolate in the fierce white light, like a cardboard town made for ghosts. No sooner were they out of sight of the housing estate than Lek turned to Samnieng and asked her:

"Do you really want to go down there?"

"Why? What were you thinking?"

"I thought we could sit under a tree and just talk."

"What about? Why can't we do it as we go along?"

She was smiling at his awkwardness but she let herself be led off the track into a small rubber plantation. It was cool and shady there and when they were in the middle of the trees Lek took the pakama* cloth that he was carrying and laid it down on the ground under one of them. Then he motioned Samnieng to sit down next to him.

"This will come out all wrong," he said after a while." Because I've never talked this way to anyone before. But I'll say it just the once and then you can think about it."

*pakama is a cotton cloth use as a towel or a sheet.

What he told her was that he had fallen in love with her and that he wanted to be with her and look after her and her children.

Samnieng spent the rest of that afternoon alone. She walked down to the village and then crossed the road and headed for the beach where she sat at the foot of one of the casuarinas that had been spared by the wave. All along the sand there was debris; shoes, clothing, toys, bottles, branches, all the wreckage left behind by the destruction. But it was good to see the spots of light dancing on the surface of the water again. She had missed this sight and even if there was still a moment of nervousness that registered in her as she stared into the clear green water she knew that she had to get back near to the sea again somehow.

On that wrecked beach shimmering in the white light Samnieng thought about what Lek had said. It had not been a total surprise because she had already guessed his feelings for her. She herself knew that while she was not in love with him she had grown very fond of him. He had been considerate to her and not tried to take advantage and she was touched by the way that he did not pressure her to make a decision. He was more than four years younger than her but he seemed mature and kind. She knew what her answer would be. How could she refuse his offer to look after her? He was a good person. That much was certain. Her daughters would have a father.

That afternoon Samnieng remained under the casuarina till it was almost dark. There had been no time for her up till then to simply sit and reflect on things, which was what she liked doing. Since the Tsunami everything had been so intense and overwhelming that each day had felt as though the wave had just struck. But Lek's words had given her back a sense of space in her heart and reminded her that she and her children and parents had survived and that there was a possibility of starting all over again. She saw quite clearly that the weeks and months and years to come would not be easy, that because of her sickness she could start to weaken at any point. But Lek seemed to be prepared for this and his gentle optimism uplifted her.

She could not understand where he got his inner strength from but she knew that it was a waste of time to try figure out such things because then she would have to ask herself all the other questions, like why so many people had been killed in the Tsunami while she and her little ones had survived, and whether it was fate or luck or karma that her illness had saved their lives by preventing her from going to work that morning. It was impossible to know. Everything was a mixed blessing. All that any of them could do was to recall for the rest of their days that they had seen the Labu manifest its terrible power and that they were still alive. If they could only do that, she thought, then they would be all right.

CLOSURE

How was it that he knew, without a doubt, that Sueb had been killed on that morning of the 26th? Was it his own projected fear of losing his lover that just happened to hit the mark on that particular occasion, or had he felt something in the depths of his heart that told, as he listened to the news of the Tsunami in the taxi, that Sueb had been swept away by the waters? Had there really been a psychic link between them, as Sueb had insisted or was it all wishful thinking?

This was one of the many conundrums that remained for Charoon in those months just after then wave struck. Of course he knew intellectually that there was no final answer to any of it and he was not by nature a person who speculated about things very deeply. In fact, like most of his compatriots he had always tended to believe that too much analysis and philosophising was unhealthy and led only to morbid depression and although he did not care much for Buddhism he had always gone along with the teaching of Aniccam, Impermanence that he had heard since childhood; simply, that things happen and you move on, that there was no point dwelling on the past. It was a line that he had applied in the forty years that he had been alive and it had usually helped him get through the painful moments in his life; the grief of losing his father and various good friends and close relatives as well as the normal run of disappointments and conflicts that are part of everyone's time on earth. But when Sueb died Charoon could not apply this attitude to come to terms with his loss. It seemed too cold and brutal.

His love for Sueb went all the way back to their intertwined childhood. They were the same age and their parents were friends and they had been taken to play together even before they could speak properly and were later sent to the same school where, more or less in the same year during their early adolescence they both discovered that they were fond of boys rather than girls; a detail which set them apart from the rest of the class as well as drew them even closer together. It was a quality they recognized in each other without any verbal discussion, like an unmistakeable reflection in the mirror and it was expressed at first in the spontaneous, innocent embraces that they managed to steal whenever they could and which gradually developed into a more intimate exploration of each other's body.

But long before they became lovers in the adult sense they were separated by circumstances. At the age of fourteen Sueb, whose father was a diplomat went abroad with his family to America and stayed there until he finished university. During this period they saw one another every two summers when Sueb visited Bangkok. They were not successful reunions. Charoon, whose own father had suffered a financial crisis and who had, as a consequence lost his business, went through a complicated phase with his childhood friend. For a start, he judged Sueb's new found farang manners as pure affectation. And then he noticed that Sueb now wanted to hang around with the other students who were being educated abroad rather than his old friends who had stayed at home. This struck him as a kind of snobbery that was both shallow and hurtful. But worst of all was that Sueb no longer seemed to want to resume or develop the intimacy they had shared when they were younger. In fact, it seemed to Charoon that his friend was trying his best to show the world that he was straight, and he could not understand the reason for this. All he knew was that it was a lie, and he felt betrayed.

By the time that Sueb was in college in America doing a degree in Business Studies and Charoon was in Thammasat studying Social Science they had more or less accepted that they now belonged to different worlds. Whenever Sueb came back to Bangkok he pursued a hectic social life. Coming from a distinguished family and being rich and good looking his moves interested the popular press and his picture was often in the magazines together with the interviews that he gave which, in Charoon's opinion showed how out of touch he had become with what was going on in Thailand. Charoon now made it a point, among their mutual acquaintances, of holding up Sueb as an example of the crassness of the foreign educated ruling class who thought that they were a cut above the rest merely because they could speak fluent English.

Nevertheless, despite his public antipathy Charoon quietly followed Sueb's progress in Thai society with keen interest. Secretly he wanted to make contact once again with Sueb and he often daydreamed of this happening in a café or the lobby of a hotel; a chance meeting that would end up with them flinging their arms round each other like before. The truth was that he felt incomplete without the friendship that they had once known.

But it was to be more than a decade before their paths crossed again. After graduating with a master's degree Sueb joined a foreign company and worked abroad in Hong Kong and Taipei while Charoon started teaching in Mahidol University and became involved in an NGO dealing with the Aids problem in Thailand. They were busy years that he would look back on as engaging but far from fulfilling. It was not for lack of companionship. Although he was not promiscuous Charoon went through a string of lovers during those years, but always with a caution that came with uncertainty, taking care not to become too involved and making sure that he was always protected both emotionally and physically. Inevitably, given his reticence none of these relationships were ever satisfying and in the end they fizzled out as a result of some episode of infidelity on his part or his partner's. During this period he thought of Sueb less and less and whenever he did it was no longer with any hope that they would ever find each other again.

One evening, just after his 38th birthday Charoon went alone to a bar off Sathorn on a whim. It had just opened and he had read somewhere that it was different, more sophisticated than the others, a good place to relax. He was curious to see what it was like and that evening he felt lonely and open to meeting any stranger who might find him attractive. But when he arrived the bar was practically deserted and he was ready to turn around and walk out again. Then looking over he saw Sueb, whom he recognized immediately, sitting alone in the corner reading a book with a drink untouched on the table in front of him. He walked up and greeted his childhood friend and from that moment on, for the next two years they were inseparable.

It was a golden time when it seemed that both of them had rediscovered their other half. Sueb, who was now based in Bangkok moved into the apartment and they were content just to be in each other's company. They did not have to talk about love or commitment. It was as though they had never been apart since they were young boys. In a moment of tenderness Sueb said that they had always been linked psychically through all the years that they had been apart and that was why they were meant to find each other again. Charoon was touched by this, but, priding himself as a rational person, was not sure whether it had any basis in reality. Yet he had to admit that the separate paths they had taken seemed to have prepared them for each other so perfectly that some days he felt that that there was nothing more to wish for in terms of passion, companionship, and contentment. He was totally fulfilled by the love that they shared.

Then one day, out of nothing came the storm; Mara materializing out of a cloud. It was jealousy that set off the chain of events. This is obvious to him now but at the time he could not see what he was doing. Mara, the trickster, blinded him with righteousness. It began with an innocuous incident. An old friend of Sueb's was visiting Bangkok and they went to have drinks with him in a hotel bar. The man, an Austrian writer, got high and tried to flirt with Sueb who did not respond.

Afterwards, when they were back home Charoon began to question him about the Austrian, which made Sueb laugh. No, there had never been anything between them, Sueb said, and Charoon could have left it like that but, unsatisfied, he persisted and interrogated Sueb about all his former lovers and past affairs. It was the first time that he had done anything like this. He could hear his own hysterical voice and the obsessive, possessive words spilling out of his mouth but there was no way that he could control them. Sueb soon lost his patience and finally stormed out leaving Charoon to brood by himself. Two days later he returned. They made love and drank whiskey and neither of them mentioned the episode again, nor where Sueb had been. But both of them knew that something had changed. Charoon was angry with himself for the distrust he had shown. But it was too late. There was now an uncomfortable tension between them.

It was Sueb who eventually suggested a change. Christmas was due in a week. They needed a break from the city and the traffic and the pollution and the crowded shopping malls filled with girls dressed like Santa Claus handing out leaflets with the foreign carols droning on in the background. He thought that they could take a trip up North, to Luang Prabang. Neither of them had been there. They could go and visit the temples and make merit for Charoon's father who had died the year before. But Charoon said that he preferred the sea. The fresh air and the swimming would do them good. Sueb gave way and agreed remembering that a cousin of his had opened a resort in the South, on the Andaman coast. It was supposedly an eco friendly place with simple bungalows right on the beach. Even though it was the high season and they had left it late to book he knew that she would find them a place to stay. So it was all settled.

But on the Friday morning, just as they were due to leave Bangkok Charoon told Sueb that he had forgotten that he had to take his mother for a check up at the hospital that weekend, and that he would follow Sueb down South on the Monday. This was a lie. The real reason was that he was panicking and needed a few days to himself. His thoughts were becoming complicated. He was sure that Sueb was still disappointed by his outburst over the Austrian and angry with him for being so unreasonable. At the time he could not help feeling that Sueb was being unnaturally kind towards him, which made him question why. He had never been paranoid like this before, nor so frightened of losing someone. It was the dangerous brew of attachment and insecurity. Yes, he can see it now. But at the time he could only watch himself freefalling into his own darkness and he knew that if he did not do something to stop it he was about to drag them both into a black hole. He needed just a few days to calm down and sort himself out.

Sueb seemed to understand what Charoon was going through and was reluctant to leave him alone. He said that he could wait, that as far as he was concerned there was no rush to leave the city particularly if it meant that he was going to be by himself. But Charoon insisted that he should go ahead, adding, without meaning to:

"Oh, I'm sure you'll find some good company down there."

In the end he had driven Sueb to the airport. They squeezed each other's hand as they parted. When he was about to go through the gate Sueb turned and waved and made a circular gesture with his forefinger and mouthed the words," See you soon", before blowing a kiss. And that was the last that Charoon ever saw of him.

He had not gone down to the ceremony that had taken place in a small temple near Baan Naam Khem. The family had decided not to ship the corpse back to Bangkok but to cremate him in the South where he had died. Afterwards Sueb's mother had given Charoon a porcelain urn containing some of her son's ashes. She also told him that she did not blame him for her son's death, and that he should not blame himself. It was a matter of karma, she said, and there was nothing anyone could do to change that.

But these words did not help. In fact, they puzzled him, and Sueb's death haunted him, and his grief was made worse by the guilty knowledge that he had sent his friend to die and that if it had not been for his feelings of insecurity they would have gone together. He realized that it was his absurd, unfounded jealousy that had saved his life.

Often, during those first months after Sueb had gone Charoon would wake up in the middle of the night from a bad dream and sit on his bed shivering. Then gradually a kind of numbness crept over him. The motivation to do anything drained away and he went about his life in a daze not caring what happened. His mother wanted him to get professional help and a therapist was contacted. But in the end he refused to go. He did not want to entrust a stranger with what was most precious to him; his memories of Sueb.

Almost a year later Charoon booked a flight to Phuket. It had taken him a whole week to summon up the strength and courage to do so. He decided that he would stay on the island and hire a car to drive up the coast to the resort where Sueb had been killed and to the temple where he had been cremated. He had only been to the South once before, as a young boy on a family holiday. But it was on the other coast, in Songkhla. On that occasion he was stung badly by a jellyfish, which probably contributed to his general distrust of the sea. He had always preferred the mountains of the North to the coast. He wondered why he had suggested that they come down South in the first place.

He arrived in Phuket on a Friday evening. The hotel he had chosen was only about twenty percent full even though it was officially the high tourist season. The staff went round with a despondent air as though they had given up expecting business to ever revive. Charoon had booked in for the weekend. It was more than enough time to accomplish the tasks that he had set for himself.

On that first evening he ate in the Italian restaurant with a terrace that overlooked the beach. There were no other guests except a young, blonde foreign couple standing on the balcony who stared at him with a look of familiarity as he entered. He noticed that the man wore a Rasta hairstyle and that both he and his girlfriend had shoulder bags with the same tribal designs embroidered on them. He thought that they were going to sit at one of the tables but after scrutinizing him for a while they turned and silently walked down the steps towards the beach and into the darkness.

During the meal he asked the girl who was serving him whether she had been there when the Tsunami hit and she told him, in a trembling voice how she had stood on one of the upper floors watching it come in and catch the people who were on the beach, how she saw children dashed against trees and buildings and how afterwards she had to walk past all the bodies which, to her amazement had all been stripped naked by the wave and how two days later when she came to help with the clean up her hair and clothes took on the scent of death which would not go away whatever she did. She stood by his table for half an hour telling her story as though it was the first time that she had a chance to do so to someone who would listen.

Perhaps it was what the girl had said but that night Charoon could not sleep even after finishing off all the liquor from the mini bar and watching three forgettable television movies. An hour or so before dawn, slightly drunk he went out onto the balcony and stared up at the half moon in a cloudless sky and wondered aloud why he had come. The action he had taken suddenly seemed absurd and vapid, What, he asked himself, was there to achieve by being there at all and visiting the site where Sueb had drowned? As he stood listening to the lapping sea and the shriek of a night owl he felt so desolate that for an instant he toyed with the idea of walking down to the beach and carrying on walking into the dark waters. But he knew that he did not have the courage nor the conviction to kill himself.

He finally got to sleep just as dawn was rising and woke only when the concierge rang him to say that the hired car had been delivered. After a shower and a quick breakfast he drove out along the West coast of the island and then over the bridge to the mainland. He had already studied the map and now he made his way fast and purposefully through the towns and small villages without paying attention to the lush vegetation that lined the road, or the green hills thick with tall trees and the big colourful birds that swooped down from them, or the wild flowers and plants that were in abundance in that area of the coastline. These were things that he would have once shared with Sueb. But alone he had no desire left to appreciate anything. He only knew that he was now determined to see the journey he had undertaken through to its conclusion.

The Rose Resort. It was a strange coincidence. The bar where he had been reunited two years earlier was called the Rose bar. The sign on the main road pointing to it was faded and could easily have been missed but Charoon, remembering Sueb's description of where it was saw it in time and turned off down the narrow, dusty track which led through the rubber plantations towards the sea.

At the end of this track he entered the grounds of the resort. Two buildings still stood; old Thai style houses that had been transported from Ayudhya and reassembled. These had previously served as the reception are and dining room. Charoon could see that there was some repair needed, but all in all they were in good shape considering what had happened. Faces peered out of the windows as he parked his car next to the three pickups that were already there. Behind the building there was what looked like the remains of a garden, a children's playground and a swimming pool, now a mess of fallen trees, broken swings, cracked tiles. Charoon had expected to see the ruins of the bungalows that lined the beach but behind the swimming pool area there was only the sand and the sea itself sparkling in the sunlight. For a moment before he could check himself he thought: " There were no bungalows. Sueb wasn't here at all. "

A man's voice from behind him said:

"What do you think? We've cleaned it up well, haven't we?"

It was as though his dark thoughts had been heard and answered. He turned to face a thin man wearing a straw hat staring at him. "We started with the bungalows. They were totally destroyed. We've taken them all down now. We'll put up the new ones in time for the next season. We'll get everything done. "

Charoon presumed correctly that he was a foreman on the site. Now they were joined by a group of young men stripped to the waist with turbans on their head to protect them from the sun. He wanted to ask more questions about the bungalows but the man had already turned to talk to his gang and was delegating the work to be done. Charoon left them and walked up to the main building and climbed the steps. At the top a young woman dressed in a traditional outfit came out to greet him.

"I hope you haven't come here to stay," she said as she bowed. And then she continued with a giggle: "As you can see, we're not ready yet. We won't be until next year."

"No,"he replied." I'm not looking for a place to stay. I wanted to come because a friend of mine was a guest here when the Tsunami struck, and he was killed."

The directness of his words made the girl's eyes widen and for a moment she was at a loss for something to say.

"Were you here then? " he went on."You might have known him.His name was Sueb."

She shook her head.

"No. I came afterwards. All of us did. We're just here to keep the place clean and answer the phone, things like that."

"So you wouldn't know..." Charoon's voice trailed off. He suddenly felt tired and muddle headed. They were now standing in the lobby, which was a wide, tastefully decorated space. He noticed a row of photographs on the wall. The girl, seeing his interest, said:

"Oh yes. They were taken by a foreign guest who stayed here, someone famous, I think. He sent them to the owner. That one there's the resort before the Tsunami. Apparently he went up in a small plane to take that picture. The one next to it was when the wave hit, and that's what it looked like afterwards."

Charoon was hardly listening to her. He had seen the images on television and in the newspapers at the time it happened. But they were not pictures of where his lover had died. These were and they focused his concentration. He stared at the "Before the Tsunami" photograph and counted twelve bungalows in rows of four, all constructed with local material in the style of the huts on that coast; the platted dry grass walls, the bamboo columns, the thatched roofs. Sueb had told him that the cousin was giving them the one right in the front row on the beach because a family from Sweden had cancelled. He wondered which one of the four Sueb had been in.

"Is the owner around today?" he asked. He had heard that Sueb's cousin had survived.

"No. She's in America. She went there to get away from everything. She'll be back soon."

When Charoon left the girl he walked down to the garden area where the builders were now beginning their day's work, then past the broken pool and into the space where the bungalows had once stood. Recalling the photograph he tried to guess the exact location in what was now an empty, neutral patch of sand. He pictured Sueb in the farthest one on the right and in his mind he visualized his old lover lying on the bed reading under the whirling fan, taking a shower, getting dressed, fixing a drink, opening the door, running into the sea laughing. Charoon choked with these visions.

He had not decided exactly what to do with the ashes he had brought along. A hundred metres or so to the South there was a fishing boat moored. He could see the fisherman's family sitting under a palm tree mending the nets. When he was a young boy his parents had hired a boat and taken his grandfather's ashes and scattered in the sea at Paaknaam, near Bangkok. He had thought of doing the same thing with Sueb's ashes but there on the beach, in sight of the boat that he might have hired he felt that he did not want to repeat an action merely because it was a custom. Sueb had once told him:

> "When we were in our teens I couldn't bear the traditions, everyone bowing to each with all that false respect. That's why I tried to be a farang for a while. But it didn't feel right either."

Charoon turned northward away from the boat and headed towards the rocks at the far end of the bay. The sun was fierce now and burning the back of his neck and his bare arms. As he walked he lifted his shoulder bag above his head as a shield. At one point the small urn containing the ashes fell out. As he bent down to pick it up he saw, there in the sand beside the urn a small rubber crocodile, about the length of his palm, its paint bleached by the salt and the sun. Charoon held it and examined it carefully. Had it belonged to a child who had been taken by the wave, he wondered.

He found a palm tree close by and sat down in its shade with the urn in one hand and the crocodile in the other. Then on impulse he put these objects on the sand, stripped off all his clothes and ran naked into the sea kicking the water and yelling out loudly as he did so.

He had expected the beach to slope down gently but when he was barely five metres away from the shore he found that he no longer had a footing. The wave had changed the contours of the seabed. It felt like stepping into an abyss. He began swimming. Looking down he could not see the bottom. A shoal of brightly coloured fish darted to his left. Then suddenly a strong undercurrent pulled him rapidly away from the shoreline. In reaction he turned his body and strengthened his strokes. But his efforts were hardly enough to keep him in the same position. Then, as fast as it had drawn him out the current began to gently push him back towards the land.

Charoon treaded water for a while when he was near the shore aware that at any moment he could be pulled out again. But he knew that he was not in danger and that there was no need to resist. As he stayed there waving his arms and legs in the warm green water he looked back towards the resort and saw the trees and all the wreckage and the space where the bungalows had been and he remembered what the waitress in the hotel had told him; that there had been five waves riding on top of each other rushing in like a monster. He wanted to believe that Sueb had not suffered, that he had been drowned in an instant.

Aung Soe Win, 12 years old.

Later when he was on the sand he lay face down at the water's edge. The sea lapped at his feet. The sun was burning his back. In a moment he was convulsed with tears. He had cried before, many times. But this was different. It was not from grief, or anger, or loss but from a sense of liberation that he had not anticipated. He had made the journey south to see where his friend had died and to tread on the sand and be washed there in the last place where Sueb had spent his final hours in order to find some sort of closure to the episode so that he could move on out of the inertia that was weighing him down. This meant, if anything, forgiveness; of himself for his stupid jealousy that had sent Sueb to his death, of Sueb for having abandoned him by dying, of the sea for its cruel destruction of life. He had wanted to make peace with what had happened. But as he lay there, his tears mixing with the wet sand he realized that this need for closure was fictional, a device to round off a story or a film. In reality there was no ending to anything and his grief could not be healed by any formal gesture and that true forgiveness would require much more than scattering ashes in the sea and mouthing a few prayers. He had to make the choice of going on or of drowning.

Six months after his trip South, at an Aids conference organized by the government Charoon met a young male nurse who was working in one of the hospices. His name was Niwat. He was fourteen years younger than Charoon and when they met he had just finished a long affair with an Englishman. At the conference they happened to be sitting next to each other and got on well from the very beginning.

One evening a couple of weeks later Charoon invited Niwat to dinner in his apartment. The first thing that the young man noticed was the photograph of Sueb on a shelf in the living room. To one side of it was a small urn and on the other a little rubber crocodile.

"He was beautiful," said Niwat as he traced the outline of Sueb's face with his finger. He had heard about Sueb already. "But what's with the crocodile?"

They laughed.

"Oh," said Charoon. " He's there to remind me that other people suffered too.

That was the first night that they made love. It felt natural and easy. Up till then Charoon was convinced that he would never want to touch or be touched by anyone else ever again. But he was glad that he was wrong and that he had found someone new. He did not feel disloyal to Sueb. No one could replace him. The time with him had been sacred. But now Niwat had come into his world and life could not stand still. It had to flow on.

THE RELUCTANT MAHOUT

No one was going to separate him from Lila now even if it meant stealing her and walking up the coast to Bangkok. They could use the trails through the forests that he had heard about from the older mahouts. There would be plenty to eat for Lila, and then when they had to use the main road he would beg for food until they reached the capitol. He had been told of mahouts and their elephants getting all the way to Bangkok from up in Surin. Why couldn't he do it from Phangnga? They would be all right once they got there. He had heard that the city was full of rich tourists and that there was a lot of money to be made every night merely by going round the bars and clubs. Farangs had a soft spot for elephants.

Of course, Ai Nok did not want to do any of this. Nor did he think that it was a realistic plan. Even if, like everyone else, he daydreamed from time to time he was not an idiot. He knew how hard it would be. The police would probably stop them the moment they hit the open road. But he was not going to be parted from Lila for anything, not now after their time together and after all that they been through in the Tsunami.

It had not always been this way. In fact, he could remember how at the beginning he had harboured bad thoughts towards her. It was not the elephant's fault, nor really his. It was just that when he left Surin he had no intention of being a mahout at all. He had come down south when Tawee, a friend from the village had written home saying that there was plenty of hotel work in the Phuket area. You just had to turn up and they hired you, no problem, Tawee had said in his boastful way. That did it for Ai Nok who had just had another fight with his father over some nonsense and who was desperate to leave the village. He had been thinking of heading for Bangkok but he did not really want to go there because he had heard bad things about getting work in the capital where there seemed to be only factory jobs, construction work or the sex industry. None of these interested him in the slightest. And then a few people he had known, including a cousin the same age as himself had come back to the village infected with Aids and had died soon afterwards. Bangkok did not attract him on any level. On the other hand the idea of being a waiter in a big hotel in Phuket seemed appealing. Not that Ai Nok had any training. He had worked in the fields and done a bit of labouring and he could read and write but that was all. Still, if what his friend said was true he was willing to learn.

So one day in late November, with money that his mother had lent him Ai Nok made his way by train and bus down to Phuket. He rented a small room near the bus station and then found his friend Tawee who was pleased to see a familiar face and listen to news from back home. He treated Ai Nok to a good meal in the market and the very next day took him to see the personnel manager of the place where he was working.

They went together into a large air-conditioned office in a big resort on the beach. Ai Nok had never seen such furniture in his life; plush sofas, marble ashtrays, a wide polished wooden table, crystal vases filled with flowers. The grandness of the setting reminded him of the soap operas that he had watched on television. He was excited by the prospect of becoming a waiter there but he had hardly been introduced by his friend when the personnel manager, a kind looking middle aged man said: "Listen. I don't want to waste your time. The truth is that we have no vacancies at all. People have been arriving from the North East every day looking for work. You should try elsewhere but I think it will be the same story. Tawee was lucky. He came at a good moment. I'd like to help you out but it's impossible."

Ai Nok was downcast and must have looked it. As they were leaving the manager called out:

"Hey. You're from Surin, aren't you?"

Ai Nok turned and nodded.

"Well, they're looking for mahouts up the coast in the Khao Lak area. There's a new elephant camp that's opened there earlier this year. Why don't you try your luck there?"

Ai Nok spent the rest of that day going from one hotel to another and being told the same thing; that there were already too many workers on the island. Here and there he was offered the most menial jobs, which he refused outright, not merely because he thought that he deserved better but because the hours were long and the pay was less than what he could have got back home as a casual labourer. By the evening his feet were aching. Finally he sat down on the beach at the south end of Patong to rest a while before going back to his room near the bus station. The sun was setting like a fat orange ball dipping into the horizon. The beach umbrellas were being folded up and put away. There were a few tourists who were still on the sand getting their massages from the dark skinned, fat masseuses who plied their trade while continuing a non-stop gossip session amongst themselves. Behind him the lights were beginning to come on in the bars and the neon signs twinkled in the twilight. Painted girls were arriving for work on the backs of noisy motorbikes. The stallholders were unloading their boxes of tee shirts and fake designer garments and shouting out greetings to each other. Young tourists strolled along wearing fashionable clothes that he had seen only in the magazines. Big, flashy cars cruised by and cold eyes peered out of the smoky windows. Ai Nok took it all in and felt a moment of confusion. Everything seemed weird and alien. It was like a film set. It was not his world. Then he turned back to the sea.

At that moment, not too far in the distance to his right he saw a huge elephant loping slowly along the shore and as it came closer he saw that it was bearing the mahout and two farang ladies who were holding onto each other's arms and laughing. Ai Nok quickly got up and walked away from there.

The sight of the elephant on the beach still annoyed him much later when he was lying on his bed thinking about what he was going to do the next day. Whatever it was, he decided, it was definitely not going to be looking for a job as a mahout. Why should the personnel manager have presumed that just because he came from Surin he would know anything about elephants? Of course he knew a few people from the village who were mahouts and there were certainly a lot of elephants in Surin. But in Nok's eyes being a mahout was just a little better than being a buffalo boy. He wanted to get as far as he could from that country stuff. He wanted a decent job that paid him enough and gave him a future, not the backbreaking slog that his parents had to endure every day of their lives with little to show for it, and certainly nothing to do with elephants.

The next days were spent systematically going round the hotels and resorts on the island and being rejected by each one of them. By the end of the week Ai Nok was thoroughly disheartened. He had exhausted the possibilities and he had nearly run out of money. The only avenues left to explore on Phuket were construction or working in a bar. Neither of them was what he wanted. Back in Surin he had been on a few building sites and hated the way that they had to slave in the boiling sun and be bossed about all day long. So that left the bar.

The next afternoon he went to a place near Kamala beach called

"The Star of Phuket" where he had heard that staff was needed. It was in a street that was full of bars, and pool halls and massage parlours. The owner, who wore a loud flower print shirt, looked him up and down.

"You're a handsome boy, young and fit too. The country type," said the man with a shrug, as though he was bored. "Yeah, you'll do. I've got work for you. But you've got to behave yourself and do what you're told. The farangs are fussy. They don't like to be ripped off."

Ai Nok knew immediately what the job was going to entail. Apart from the fact that he had never done that kind of thing before and just the thought of it put him off he had made a promise to his mother that he would not land up in the sex trade. So without a word he walked out of the bar.

In the end Ai Nok borrowed some money from Tawee and caught a bus to Khao Lak.After asking around he was directed to the "Dream Elephant Camp" which was situated two kilometres up the hill from the main road. He walked along the dirt track with his bag slung over his shoulder and by the time he arrived he was covered in dust and sweat.

"So you've come all the way from Surin," said the owner, Khun Opart, a short, jovial, fat man who wore a heavy gold ring set with a red stone.

" I expect you know something about elephants."

Ai Nok told him candidly that he had never had anything to do with them.

"Ah, but it's in your blood. I'm sure of it. Anyway, if you want the job you can start right away. It's not difficult. The elephants have already been well trained. You'll be helping another mahout and it will take you no time at all to learn what to do. The basic pay is 3,500 baht a month, and I give you your board and lodging. If you want to go out and get laid, that's your own business. But I'm certainly not going to pay for that."

He paused to laugh at his own joke.

"When you can handle an elephant properly you'll be taking the tourists for a ride and then you'll be making good money from their tips. They all love an elephant ride."

Ai Nok, against his better judgment, took the job. That very day he was given a room and two sets of clothing; indigo dyed tops and trousers in the style of the traditional mahouts in the central plains.

The "Dream Elephant Camp" was smaller than most of the other camps along the coast. There were only eight elephants and sixteen handlers. Khun Opart had bought the business from a Chinese tour operator and it was doing well. Guides brought visitors up from the resorts to go trekking into the national park that lay only a few kilometres further up the track. This was the job of the more experienced mahouts as it entailed going through narrow trails, dense vegetation and crossing rivers. The younger ones mainly worked on the coast itself. The elephants were led down every morning to a meeting point next to the main road where they waited to be hired.

The man Ai Nok was assigned to apprentice with was called Nai Laab, fifty years old and originally from Ayudhya who had been a mahout since his teens. Ai Nok's first job was to clean the stables where the elephants slept. This was, for him a bad dream come true. He had always dreaded the thought of cleaning up elephant shit and now, to his utter disgust he found that there was plenty of it. In the afternoon, during the camp's rest period he was given lessons on how to mount and control the elephant. Nai Laab was a patient teacher whose experience was obvious and the elephants themselves, as Khun Opart had said, were already skilful in following the commands. All that Ai Nok had to do was to learn how to give those commands. This was done by tapping the ears with a stick, applying pressure with his feet and uttering some special sounds that the elephant seemed to understand. All these things came naturally to him. In fact, he took to the training with such ease that within two weeks of being employed Ai Nok was ready to take an elephant for a ride by himself. But before he did this he had to undergo a small initiation ceremony that was conducted by Nai Laab himself. Part of this consisted in learning a mantra that was the secret of all the mahouts. After this he became a fully-fledged member of the fraternity. To the other young men this was considered an honour. But to Ai Nok it did not feel as though he had achieved anything. On the contrary, he felt that he was now trapped in a position that he would rather have avoided. Becoming a mahout was only a little better than being a peasant.

Khun Opart and Nai Laab decided between them that Lila, a seven year old female would be good for Ai Nok to start on. She was one of the most popular elephants in the camp. She had been trained young and not only was she obedient but she was so sure footed that she could practically manage without a mahout at all. Every tourist who had been carried by her through the forest trail had come back full of praise after the ride. Lila was, in fact a faultless creature and bore the marks that impressed the trained eye of the older mahouts. This was something that Ai Nok did not appreciate in the first months that he was with her. To him she was just another dumb giant like the others, a creature trained to work and perform stupid tricks for the tourists. This was what he had seen in his native Surin.

So in the beginning, partly because of this negative attitude and partly because he was nervous about his ability to handle her after so short an apprenticeship he would dig his feet into her neck or strike her harder than he needed to and he would sometimes curse her under his breath. Lila never reacted to any of this but continued to be obedient and gentle towards her new mahout. It was as if she knew that he needed

Aekkapong Navarak 10 years old.

a while to change his ways. And little by little as the months went by she began to win his respect. Many times, crossing the busy main road or going through a village she would show him how quickly she could read a situation, anticipate the danger and respond to it, often displaying her agility in such a way that it left him speechless. Later, when they began to take the tourists trekking in the forest it was as though she was silently teaching him how to direct her and make sure that their journey was safe. In the end Ai Nok's initial resistance evaporated. He grew fond of Lila and was grateful that she had been chosen for him. Being in close proximity to her day in day out he began to recognize her individuality, her preferences and her sense of humour which she would display when it was bathing time. Eventually a friendship that he had not expected developed between them. Through Lila he saw that the whole art of handling an elephant was challenging and fascinating, not least because he came to understand how powerful the creatures were and how, if they chose, they could pick any of the mahouts up and toss him in the air without so much as a thought. It puzzled him why they chose to obey.

Gradually Ai Nok settled into the routine of his new life. There were still moments, of course when he dreamed of finding a job in some hotel in Phuket and of wearing a crisp, clean uniform and of serving at a table in a fine, fancy dining room. But he knew that he could not complain about where he had landed. Khun Opart looked after him well. He was fed free of charge, had money in his pocket and the work was not as terrible as he had imagined.

A year after he arrived in Khao Lak things had changed considerably in the area. The developers had been proved right in their decision to expand their business up the coast from Phuket. Every new venture was going from strength to strength. To the consternation of the environmentalists new tracks of forest were being carved away to make room for more resorts and the unspoiled beaches were no longer unspoiled. But no body except them were complaining. Tourists were now pouring into the area. There was hardly a difference between the high and low season any more. At the "Dream Elephant Camp"Khun Opart had bought another ten elephants and there were now double the number of staff to tend to them. The winter months were going to be so full of visitors that the resorts were already overbooked. It was a fat period for everyone, including Ai Nok. He had never made so much money in his life. The tourists were encouraged to give to the mahouts and they did this generously. Some months he made easily more than five times his basic salary. He was able to send money home to his mother with plenty left to buy the clothes and shoes that he had always dreamed of having. Not that he had much time to strut around in them. Sunday was his only day off and he was usually too tired from the week's work to want to go into town. Some of his friends liked going out to a karaoke bar but Ai Nok preferred sitting around having a beer with Nai Laab and watching a game of football on television.

The truth was that he had come to enjoy his work more than anything else. On Saturdays he and Lila would be stationed at the meeting point near the beach and take the tourists for walks along the main road up the hill to the next bay or along the track that ran parallel to the beach. He always earned well from these short stints but they were not really satisfying. What he liked were the weekdays when he would take visitors along the forest trails up to the waterfall and back. There was a trip that took two hours and a longer one when four or five elephants would go together which took half a day to do. The trails were well trodden but every time Ai Nok would come across something new that he had not noticed before; giant butterflies, wild orchids bursting from the trunk of a teak tree, eagles, snakes, monkeys. He had never imagined how rich and wonderful nature could be. In Surin the agricultural land had been harsh, the planting of rice and other crops gruelling work. He had always looked at the countryside as a place to get away from. But here in the South, for the first time in his life he felt embraced by nature's lush beauty and often during those treks he would smile to himself knowing that he was doing something extraordinary, with a great guide in the form of Lila who did not put a foot wrong, and that he was being paid a huge amount of money for it.

On the morning that the Tsunami hit he was on duty even though it was a Sunday. Khun Opart said that he would pay him overtime and he had agreed because he could not think of anything better to do that day and he knew the tips would be flowing in. He had not woken up too early and he had taken Lila down at a leisurely pace. There was a stall near the meeting point where he was going to have a bowl of rice gruel and a cup of coffee before starting the day's work. He was sure that no one would be coming until at least nine thirty. The tourists normally got up late. Only families with small children were out early.

At the meeting point he tied Lila to a wooden post. It was not really necessary as he knew that she would not go anywhere without him. But this was part of their standard procedure.

Usually she stood still as if she was meditating while she waited for him to untie her then lead her to the wooden platform where the waiting clients would climb onto the seat on her back. But that morning she seemed restless and upset, which was not like her. Ai Nok had already noticed this at the camp before they even set off. Now she was scraping the earth with her left foot and she kept raising her trunk into the air as though she was sensing something with it. He had never seen her behave like this before and he could not understand why. He took his time eating his breakfast and drinking his coffee, glancing over towards her every now and again. Perhaps she would calm down if the other elephants were there. But no one else from the camp had arrived. He guessed that they had been in the town that night to get drunk. Too bad, he thought. More work for me.

By the time that he had finished Lila was weaving her head from side to side a gesture of refusal. It now occurred to him that maybe she was ill and uncomfortable. The idea of taking her back to the camp crossed his mind and he walked up to her, stroked her trunk and said:

"Hush. What's wrong with you?"

Their eyes met and he was sure that she was trying to tell him something. Then he remembered that she had once given him the same look when he had climbed off her in the forest. They were near a river. Her look had been to warn him that there was a deadly green pit viper close to his foot and about to strike. But that he morning he could not see where the danger was coming from so he decided that it was to do with the time of the month; a moment of excitement on her part.

"Don't worry," he told her with a laugh. "That bull elephant will be waiting for you when we get back."

But by now she was beginning to shift from one foot to the other in an agitated fashion. Then without warning she raised her trunk and roared out a call. It sounded like a ship's horn blasting the air. Then, to Ai Nok's surprise a few seconds later it was answered by similar calls that seemed to come from along the whole length of the coastline. Even though he had no experience of hearing such sounds Ai Nok knew without a doubt that they were cries of anguish.

Lila began to tug at the rope that was binding her leg to the wooden stake, gently at first then with great force so that the stake was swaying and would have broken had Ai Nok not stepped up and shouted at her.

" Stay still! Stay still! I'll untie you."

Lila obeyed him and went silent for a moment while he bent down and quickly loosened the rope. Then he put his foot on her trunk and she hauled him up onto her back in one flowing movement. Now without waiting for his command she set off briskly in the opposite direction to the sea back towards the camp. Ai Nok had no time to figure out what was happening. But suddenly he heard behind him the sound of people shouting and screaming. Turning round he saw a crowd running away from the beach and behind them a wall of water, like the white head of some sea monster coming in fast. Without thinking what it was, nor remembering what he had heard about Tsunamis he knew only that there was danger. Touching Lila's left ear he shouted to her:

"Lila! We must go back. People need us."

He repeated this several times but the elephant seemed to pay him no heed and raced away from the sea. And then suddenly she stopped and wheeled her huge body round.

That morning they picked up four people; two women and two children, all locals who were running away from the wave and who had lost their strength by the time that Ai Nok and Lila reached them. All four clambered up, squeezed into the seat and clung to each other as Lila ran over the main road and scrambled up the hill to the camp. She had saved their lives.

As the following high season approached there was a sense of depression in the "Dream Elephant Camp". After the Tsunami business had plunged dramatically everywhere in the region and there was as yet no real sign that it was going to pick up despite what the government officials were telling the press. The farangs who had lost their loved ones were not going to be back at least for a while. New potential visitors were scared of a repeat. Asian tourists were afraid of the ghosts that were still around. The government's efforts to revive the tourist industry did not seem to be yielding any positive results. Up and down the coast it was more or less the same story. Even the top end resorts were seeing only a trickle of visitors returning. Rebuilding was well under way but the beaches continued to look messy as though the wave had struck the day before. There was rubbish and debris everywhere. The temporary housing estates were still full of people who had lost their homes but who did not have the proper papers that would allow them access to the new houses that the government had built. Not that these were all desirable either, it seemed. Many of these new dwellings were uninhabitable, more like concrete ovens than houses. Some of them lacked the basics such as toilets and electricity. In the rush to show that there was a program of rehabilitation to revive the area many things had been simply overlooked or half done and as a result the projects were carried out shoddily. And, as always those at the bottom of the ladder were the ones who suffered the most.

In this respect the employees of the "Dream Elephant Camp, at least for the time being, had less to complain about than many others in the tourist sector. For while people were getting laid off and finding themselves with no means of survival the mahouts still had shelter and food and many of them had earned well that year up until the Tsunami so that if they had not been too reckless and had managed to put a little aside they were all right for a while. Still, even for them the situation was becoming precarious as the days went by. Khun Opart had told them that he could no longer afford to keep the business going and that he was already looking for a company to take it over, perhaps one of the bigger set ups in Phuket. This would, of course result in a reorganization of the camp and he could not guarantee their futures. It was more than likely that the business would be scaled down, which would mean that only the experienced mahouts would be sure of continuing to be employed.

There was a lot of talk among them. Ai Nok, like the others was marking time. All he wanted was to stay with Lila. One day Nai Laab told him that he had been offered a new job in Krabi where an NGO had set up a place where old and sick elephants could be looked after. All of them in the camp had heard about this organization because every now and then their members had come round to check up on how the elephants at the "Dream Elephant Camp"were being treated. Ai Nok's views were influenced by some of the other mahouts who really hated this NGO. They were angry that their members always came unannounced like secret police and they resented the fact that their work was evaluated and judged by a bunch of busy bodies. It was common knowledge that several camps along the coast had had to close down as a result of the bad press they received after these visits. The "Dream Elephant Camp" had always passed the test but even so the NGO was definitely not popular there. And now Nai Laab was going to join them. Ai Nok's mentor was going over to the enemy.

He felt sad about this but showed no emotion when Nai Laab invited him to do the same. Nai Laab was either unaware of the effect that his decision had on the young man or he was simply choosing to ignore it. He insisted that he wanted Ai Nok to consider the proposition seriously.

"It's easier work than being here. That's for sure," he said. "But you can't expect to be paid like you're used to. The tourists go there to help out. You won't get any tips. It's a job for those who are really dedicated to elephants and who love nature."

Ai Nok told Nai Laab that he would think about it but in is heart he thought that it was the last thing that he wanted to do.

One afternoon as he was hosing Lila down a van drove up to the camp. It was from one of the resorts nearby. Ai Nok recognized the logo painted on the side door. He saw Khun Opart approach the vehicle with

an unctuous, ready smile. It was the first time in a week
that anyone had driven up there. Ai Nok wondered
how many guests had come in the van. At the same
time he knew that there was only a slim chance of him
getting a job that day. Lila was still wet and there were
other mahouts in line ready to take the guests out for
a ride. But he saw only one person step out of the van.

She was tall and wore a colourful long skirt, dark
glasses and a wide brimmed straw hat. It was hard to
tell her age but she was not young. He noticed too tat
she had a leather bag slung over her shoulder. Khun
Opart was talking to her now. Ai Nok saw her laugh
and shake her head. Then she said something else
and he was pointing over in his direction and to his
surprise they were walking over towards him. Behind
them the van driver followed. When they reached him
Khun Opart signalled for Ai Nok to turn off the hose.

"This lady wants to meet Lila," he said, adding,
slightly annoyed." I haven't a clue why. She
doesn't want a ride. I don't know what the hell
she's here for."

The woman did not understand what Khun Opart
was saying, nor did she seem to take any notice of him.
She stood looking at Lila admiringly and her trunk
with the back of her hand before stroking it. She then
turned and stared at Ai Nok. Next she spoke in English
to the driver who was by then standing with them. The
man was obviously a translator and guide as well as
a driver.

"Mrs. Miller wants to know," he said." If you have always been Lila's mahout."

Ai Nok at first shook his head and then nodded.

" I've been with her for a year and a half, almost every day."

The man translated this for the foreign woman. Ai Nok saw that she was pleased to hear it. Then she took out from her leather shoulder bag a silver picture frame and handed it to Ai Nok who looked at it and after a while smiled and nodded because he recognized the two people in the photograph. He even remembered the boy's name. It was Robert, and the woman was his mother. They had come by six days consecutively because the boy had enjoyed the rides so much. Another driver from the resort had explained to Ai Nok that both mother and son had a swim before breakfast and then the boy could not wait to get into the van to come and see Ai Nok and Lila. During a whole week he had taken them on all the forest trails and down to the sea and along the beach. The boy, Robert had told him through an interpreter that he wanted to be a mahout like Ai Nok when he was older and his mother had laughed.

Mrs. Miller now told him that she was the boy's grandmother and that every evening when she called them from England all that Robert could talk of was Lila the elephant and Nok the mahout. Mrs. Miller went on to explain that she was there in the area because she wanted to see where her daughter and grandson had been. The holiday had been her idea. They had come through a tough time. Her daughter had recently divorced from Robert's father. The boy was suffering from a depression. They needed a change of air. It was going to be a Christmas treat that she paid for. She was meant to have come with them but in the end she had another commitment that forced her to delay her journey. She had planned to join them later in Bangkok.

As the driver translated her words Ai Nok noticed that she was trying to hold back her tears. He knew why because he had found out, from the sister of another mahout who worked in the resort, how Mrs. Miller's daughter and grandson had been swept away by the wave on the morning of the Tsunami and that their bodies had been found near each other at the foot of a hill nearby. The news had made him sad at the time because he had liked Robert and had been infected by the boy's enthusiasm for everything that he saw and touched. They had communicated with each other through gestures and through laughter. Robert had been very fond of Lila and his mother, for her part had been generous to him with her tips; so much so, in fact that sometimes he had felt embarrassed to receive them.

Mrs. Miller asked how things were at the camp because she had heard that times were tough. Ai Nok let Khun Opart answer this. He told her that they would probably be closing if they could not find a buyer because he could no longer afford the monthly wages and the elephants were too expensive to maintain. Business was picking up in Phuket but where they were it was going to take at least another year. He had debts. He could not afford to wait. Mrs. Miller nodded as she took in the information.

"And what will you do if you have to leave?" she said this turning towards Ai Nok." Will you go on with this work somewhere else?"

When he understood her question Ai Nok suddenly felt the doubt drop away from his heart.

"Yes," he replied." I will always be a mahout and I want to look after Lila".

Mrs. Miller nodded again. When it was time to leave she shook his hand warmly and made the driver translate one last thing for her.

"Tell him," she said slowly as though she wanted the translator to convey her exact meaning." Tell him that he and Lila healed my grandson. I know they did. And for that I will be eternally grateful."

Four days later she and the same driver drove up to the camp once more. This time she insisted on talking to Ai Nok without Khun Opart being present. She told him that she had finished what she had come to do and that she was going to leave now for Bangkok and then on to England. She was sure that she would not be back. She had made enquiries during her stay. She knew how bad things were in that area and that it was likely to get even worse, at least in the short term. As they said goodbye she handed him, without the driver seeing, a plain white envelope.

"Thank you," she said as she climbed into the van. Ai Nok slid the door shut and in a second it was disappearing down the dusty track.

That evening when he was alone in his room Ai Nok counted out what she had given to him. It was a big sum of money. He lay on the bed and thought about what he could do with it. He had worried about money all his life and he had always daydreamed about having the means to set himself up in some small business such as having his own taxi or pickup back in Surin. The amount she had given him was enough to do this.

But then he remembered Lila.

When he rode through the gates with Lila into "The Sanctuary" Nai Laab was the first person to greet him because his young acolyte had already phoned to tell him that he was coming. Ai Nok and Lila had walked all the way down the coast. Both of them were tired and hungry.

"Well?" said the older man, his eyes laughing.

"Seeing as you've brought your elephant, are you ready to work now? Are you going to be a true mahout? Ai Nok smiled, nodded and stroked Lila's head. It felt like he was home.

THE FINAL MESSAGE

Charoon, my dearest friend, I know that you are not as yet aware that you have freed me and allowed me to move on. I feel that it is important to tell you how this came about and this is why I am writing to you now. There are things I'm going to say that I have not told you before and I am aware that they may hurt you. But this is not my intention. If anything I want you to know that you were right in your suspicions. They had no basis at the time but I can see now that I would have ended up hurting you in the way that you imagined. In any case I am glad that you too have moved on. Even if I have no idea where it is I am heading, or, in fact if there is a destination at all I am ready for the journey I am about to take.

It is curious that this is the last thing that I am doing; typing out these words. As a boy I wanted to be a writer. I had so many stories in my head but I always found, when it came to writing them down that I could start them off but never finish them. Lack of focus, as one of my teachers said. Then later there were so many excuses not to write at all, such as studying for a degree, then training for a career that had little to do with literature. By the time I was in my twenties the idea of writing fiction had been pushed into the background with very little chance of ever being revived. (We talked about this issue once, I remember, when we were discussing how different our lives might have been if we had pursued our passions). And now as I am about to leave I feel ready once more to tell a story, without the pressure of having to finish or even to begin.

When you receive this you will immediately be asking how it is possible that I am able to write this message to you at all since you know beyond any doubt that I died that day the Tsunami struck and that the ashes you were given by my mother after the cremation are the remains of my earthly body. So I will begin by telling you I am one of those phenomena called ghosts. I can hear your disbelieving laughter. The last time we talked about the subject was when that story in the newspaper that everybody was excited about came out. Do you remember? It was about a monk who, after his death, appeared to his ex disciples and told them that there was treasure hidden in the temple grounds. You, sceptical as always, dismissed the whole subject. It was rubbish, you said, and the fact that most of our compatriots subscribed to the existence of ghosts only showed how gullible they were. And yet I am the (I was going to say "living") proof that may convince you once and for all that ghosts do exist.

Let me explain.

On that day, the 26th December 2004 I was drowned by the Tsunami wave and my physical body died. But I did not die; that is to say, to my amazement I found myself still inhabiting the same dimension that you are in, but as a disembodied shadow of energy, conscious of existing but without having a form or being bound by the physical reference points that I had previously know; a ghost, in other words.

Let me give you more details as I know that for many months, and probably even now you have been wondering about them.

On that morning of the 26th I woke up at 8.30. It was earlier than usual given that I was on holiday. But I was alone, as you know and I had not drunk anything the night before nor watched hours of television as I usually do when I find myself away from home, simply because there was no telly in that bungalow. I had swum a lot the day before and I was tired. So it had been a good restful sleep from which I awoke refreshed. I did not want to have breakfast straightaway, nor did I want to have a swim. I prefer the water in the evening. So in the end I decided to go for a walk along the bay. Stepping out of the bungalow and directly onto the sand I felt a strange moment of apprehension as I looked at the sea. There was something about the milky texture of its surface, which had been so clear and transparent the day before. But it passed and I thought no more about it and walked up the beach towards the rocky headland that separated that bay from the next one. About a hundred metres on I saw a boat that had come in from the night's catch. A family was beside it; two women tending to the nets, two men unloading the catch and a boy sitting in the sand watching them. As I approached I could hear them arguing. At least that is what I thought they were doing from their animated voices and their gestures. They spoke very fast in the

Southern dialect and I did not understand a word of what they were saying. They hardly glanced at me as I walked past them. Only the boy looked around. As soon as I reached the rocks I started to turn back.

At that point I thought of you and wondered if you were really going to join me as you had promised or whether you were going to carry on punishing me by staying in Bangkok. We had just gone through our first crisis. You had not even called, knowing very well that this would worry me as in the two years that we had been together we had called each other at work two or three times a day.

I am still trying to figure out how it was that you suddenly realized that my commitment to you was not equal to your love for me. This was the real reason for your jealousy, wasn't it? I know now that I should have come clean and admitted this instead of letting you go on thinking that you were crazy and paranoid. So I am now telling you that you were right in thinking that I had betrayed you, because, even if I had done nothing at that point in our relationship I knew that I was capable of it at any moment. This is not something I want to defend. It has always been my nature. But you must have known too that I was not lying when I told you that ours was the closest relationship that I had ever had and that the link between us that has bound our lives since childhood was a real one that I can still feel.

Anyway, all these thoughts were going round my head and by the time I got back to the bungalow it seemed a good idea to have a shower and put on fresh clothes before going round to the breakfast room. The bathroom of the bungalow was half open to the sky. No doubt my cousin thought that this would make the guests feel even closer to nature. From where I stood in the bathing area I had a clear view of the sea. That morning I had my back to the window and I was humming a Cole Porter tune.

It was the roar that made me turn around. And then all at once the white wall of water was on top of me.

Was there pain? Did I suffer? This has worried you, hasn't it? Yes. For one brief second when my body was smashed against the wall there was a physical implosion for which nothing could have prepared me. But then something happened so fast that even now when I look back I cannot capture it. It was like suddenly slipping out of the skin. Plop. Just like that. And there I was accompanying my body in the torrent of water. I watched it being broken against a tree and then crashing into a car that was floating by and then carried inland past huts and boats and fences until I saw myself lying face downward on the other side of the main road. In all of this passage I felt nothing. I was beside my body, moving with it but not inhabiting it. When the water finally subsided my corpse, naked and bruised lay in a piece of open ground. There were many other bodies nearby and I noticed other shadows standing over them as I was. But the curious thing was that there were not as many shadows as there were corpses and this immediately made me ask myself what was happening, why I was still there. Soon people came up and began loading the dead bodies very carefully into the back of trucks. I accompanied mine to a temple on a hill nearby.

I will spare you the details. I know that my mother must have told you of the way they finally identified me, and about the cremation that you did not attend that hot afternoon. The strange thing about that episode was that I could really feel the power of the prayers and all the chanting encouraging me to leave and continue my journey out of this world of Dukkha*. And for my part I was perfectly willing to do so. But I could not go anywhere. That was the problem. I was stuck without understanding what it was that was holding me back.

I had always thought that a ghost was a trace of someone with some deep unresolved attachment at the time of his or her death. I remember in my childhood hearing of the ghost of a beautiful young woman who was often seen at the corner of the street near our house. Apparently she had been stabbed to death by her husband while she was waiting for her lover. People in the area regularly lit candles and incense for her by the tree near where the incident had happened. Everyone said that her karma had been too abruptly cut short. I thought I understood what they meant. But in my own case I could not identify anything that might have kept me in this suspended condition. (Does that, I wonder,

Dukkha means suffering.

say something about the lack of intensity of my love for you? I have given this a lot of thought and my conclusion is that it cannot be so because there were surely others who loved as passionately as we did and were still able to pass on).

As for the shock factor, I cannot really understand why I should have stayed on while many who were also taken completely by surprise that morning should have managed to leave. I have to admit that during that first period of my existence as a ghost these questions preoccupied me and I felt a certain sense of injustice in being one of those who were still around. But gradually, faced with the fact that there seemed to be no escape and no logic to my absurd predicament I began to become fascinated by my state and to feel more and more at home in the new landscape in which I found myself. Of course I am using the same old syntax and the same words to describe this. But even the term " I" is inadequate, as one of the first things that you notice when you are a ghost is that the "I" you once were, which was defined by your needs and desires has ceased to have meaning. The body no longer binds you. None of the sensual limitations compel you; no hunger, no thirst motivates you any more. The physical world does not hinder your movements. You pass through closed doors and brick walls without effort. And yet I did notice from the beginning that there was a clear geographical boundary to my ghostly existence. At a certain radius from where the wave took me I would start to come against an invisible veil that prevented me from going any further and a sort of longing would come over me. I learned that my patch went as far north as Kuraburi and as far south as Krabi, but I never understood why this should be so.

How did I pass all those months which now seem like the blink of an eye? I know that when you read this message this will be one of the first questions that will arise because you know how difficult it was for me to do nothing. You accused me of being a workaholic -a term I did not like at all. But there was truth in it. Looking back I see that I kept busy in my life to stave off the melancholy and depression that I had known since I was a boy. So it will surprise you to know that as a ghost, without any task at hand to keep me occupied I was quite content to pass my time watching and observing all the hectic activity that came after the wave; the medical teams, the army, the government officials, the NGO's and the foreign volunteers, the visiting politicians and the performers and their entourage trying to whip up enthusiasm for the resurgence of tourism and business in the area. And then there were the people who survived in these parts still looking as though the wave has just hit. I have seen so much grief and suffering, and sheer shock. Yet what has touched me is how resilient (we) humans are, how after such a horrific event people manage to carry on.

During this time the question of why I was still here still continued to puzzle me now and then and I sought the answer by trying to see what similarities I shared with my fellow ghosts who were wandering along this coastline. There are a substantial number and I have come to recognize most of them. I was curious to learn why they too were unable to leave. But I never found out because there seem to be no way that ghosts can communicate beyond a vague, fleeting sense of empathy that arises whenever we pass by each other. Sometimes a nod would be exchanged to signify, I suppose an understanding of each other's condition. But the truth is probably that we don't. What surprised me, though, was that there was none of the psychic exchanges that I had imagined. I saw the others wandering about like me passing through walls, gliding between cars, sitting in seelaws, lying under trees on the beach. The children looked beautiful, often surrounded by a kind of radiance.

As for being perceived by those who are alive, it remains a mystery to me exactly what happens. There seems to be people who are more sensitive to seeing us than others. And to these we appear during certain periods of the day or night when the parameters of so-called reality become less defined. This has something to do with the light, I am sure; the purple twilight and the dreamy glow of the moonlight exert a strong influence. And yet it is impossible to say precisely what happens. I can only tell you that as far as I am concerned it corresponds to a moment of deep nostalgia, a yearning to recover the senses again, to feel desire and pain once more. And then it happens. I can then actually feel a kind of heaviness, reminiscent of when I still had a solid body and experienced the pull of gravity. If at this moment there happens to be a sensitive person nearby he or she sees me.

Once I was back on the beach where I was drowned and I saw the same family by their boat in almost the same place they had been that morning of the Tsunami. It was early evening and there was a green and golden light in the sky. The men were on the boat, the women were working with the nets and the boy was playing in the sand. I was glad to see that they had all survived the wave. The boy looked up as I went by. He pointed at me and spoke some words. The rest of his family stopped what they were doing and followed his gaze. But I knew that they could not see me; only the boy could.

Theera Khongthip, 12 years old.

Now because time is running out I want to come to the day when you visited the resort because it was when I began to understand my condition more clearly. Had I been expecting you to come? The short answer is yes, I was, knowing that being who you are you had to make the journey South at some point. You have to feel that things are neatly finished off. You like closure. I have to say that I was surprised you were not there at the cremation but I realized that you were grieving in your own way. After that I waited patiently to see you again. Please understand that this was not an obsession on my part. Unlike the young woman on the street corner in Bangkok I was not pining for my lover to come back to me. I was merely curious to see how you were. After all we have known one another all our lives.

Then you made your decision and I sensed that you were coming. I made my way up the coast from Phuket where I had been hanging around watching a parade. That day I saw you arrive and talk to the people in the main building and then walk along the beach with my ashes in your bag. I saw the urn fall out and you bending down to pick it up and finding the crocodile buried I the sand. I had seen that toy several times before and also wondered where it came from, who had been its owner. I was glad that you took it. Then later when you were in the sea I was there beside you.

I was happy to see you again lying there naked in the sand. It was not the nakedness but the spontaneity with which you had thrown off your clothes. You were always so modest about your body. You never felt that you were beautiful enough for me. It 's true, isn't it? I stood over you and watched you lying there faced downward with the sun burning your back. Then suddenly you started to cry and it was in that moment that I understood that the reason I could not move on was because your attachment to me was so solid and unshakeable. I realized that it was you who had to let go, you who had to cut the cord that bound us together. The knot had been tightened by what had happened between us before our last parting, and also by your guilt at having survived me. Suddenly it was all clear to me. But how was I to communicate all of this to you? I could only trust that in time you would arrive at a point when you could let me go without feeling disloyal to our memory. I told you many times that I thought we had a special link to each other which could not be explained and you always pretended to agree with me although I knew that you saw this merely as a poetic way of expressing my closeness to you. But now you can see that it was not wishful thinking on my part.

Last night I sensed beyond all doubt that you were in someone else's arms, making love with him. In my other life this might have been something I intuited that would have made me jealous. But I knew that I was not wrong because I became aware that my presence was diminishing, that your attachment to me was unravelling, and I realized that it was the beginning of the end of my time as a ghost. As your energy draws away from me so mine begins to fade. You desire and affection towards your new lover will grow and soon

I will disappear completely. The process has already started and I have no regrets about it, only gratitude.

The night manager left the computer switched on while he went off to sleep with a maid in one of the spare rooms. I seized my chance without knowing how I would manage it. I spent a long time with my ghostly fingers over the keyboard without making contact. Then it occurred to me to focus on the love that I have for you and to trust that its energy can transcend time and distance. It felt so simple and effortless. The screen came alive!

So this is the end of my message. I have used up my strength and my love writing this to you and it will soon be dawn. I am happy to go. All that remains is for me to press "send" in my mind and these words will be carried into space to you. We can both be free.

AFTERWORD

On the tenth anniversary of the Indian Ocean tsunami that took place on 26 December 2004 I was interviewed for the magazine section of the Bangkok *Post*, on the strength of having written *After the Wave*. The questions were sent to me by email and I had time to ponder them carefully before offering my replies. In the process of doing so I was curious to know how the event had been recorded and written about by individuals and organisations in the intervening years. So I started trawling the Internet. The subject of the tsunami would come up in a conversation now and again, particularly in the family because of the circumstances that led to us just miss being down on the Andaman coast when the waves struck. But it had been ages since I had revisited that time of my life so directly. As I went through the sites I found the best report regarding the tragedy and the lessons to be learned from it was published by the Oxfam research team in December 2014. The figures still stagger me: 227,000 dead; millions of others whose lives have been shattered. I came across only a few personal testimonies but their effect was devastating. As for the images, I had seen the footage that appeared in the news coverage at the time but I had not seen many of the home movies and videos that had been compiled since then, nor the photos from the countries that were affected. They too have retained their power to shock.

Going back over this old ground I found the memory of my days spent in the south of Thailand – from early 2005 till about a year and a half later – still startlingly vivid, and I realized how profoundly my involvement in the tsunami's aftermath shaped my direction since then. It was already an emotionally intense period in my life. In between the trips from Bangkok to Phuket I was looking after my mother, who was entering the final year of her Alzheimers. I was also working as a volunteer in a hospice in the Klong Toey slums where adults and children with full-blown Aids came to be looked after, many of them eventually to die there with us. The role of carer was not one that came naturally or easily to me. When the tsunami struck and the People Living with Aids (PLWA) group invited our team from the Mercy Centre in Bangkok to go down and help them we could not predict what we would find, or what we could do to help. This was a disaster on a scale so immense that no one had ever seen the likes of it.

A doctor said to me recently: 'Be present at a birth and at a death and you don't need any other teaching.' She meant that by being present at those two key moments we would value what it is to be human and stop fighting one another. I agreed with her, yet there was no time to extend our conversation. But afterwards I remembered how one of my university economics tutors, disgruntled with the continuing injustices and inequalities in the world and the failure of political ideologies to provide any meaningful answer had once remarked: 'In the end only a disaster will change us.' It seemed a callous thing to say. But he explained that to him an environmental catastrophe, with all the terrible suffering that it implied, was the only way we would wake up and act collectively, forgetting our differences, help those in need and transcend our usual self-centred interests. I recalled his words in relation to the tsunami's aftermath. For this was what I saw firsthand: basic human kindness, sacrifice and selflessness beyond the divisions created by dogma and ignorance — the true compassion that followed in the wake of the tragedy when the barriers had been levelled. A hard lesson. So, in answer to the good doctor perhaps I might have said: Birth, death, and confronting suffering firsthand.

In Khao Lak the suffering that gave rise to the compassion was everywhere. Through the years, whenever I think about that tsunami and what it left behind I always remember the fisherman I'd spent time with. He had been separated from his wife when the waves crashed in. After the waters subsided he wandered around in a daze looking for her, praying that she would be alive, eventually finding her in one of the makeshift morgues that had been set up in a local school. Crazy with grief he put her corpse in the plastic tub he used to transport his catch to the markets along the coast. He covered her body in salt water, as he would the fish, and put the tub in the back of his pickup truck. He drove nonstop to her village in the northeast, taking her back to the place where she was born. The pain of loss that he and others shared with me and my colleagues who were working there to help the survivors moved me deeply, and today I pray that time has helped to heal him and those whose lives were overturned by the waters. In the middle of the sadness I was also profoundly moved by the sheer resilience of the people I met and that too has remained with me. And, apart from the human aspect, I was awestruck by the force of the elements, manifest in the physical destruction along the coast: crushed buildings, twisted and broken trees, beaches littered with human paraphernalia such as shoes, bits of clothing, toys. One morning after arriving in Khao Lak, the area that had been one of the hardest hit, I swam out in the emerald green sea just as the sun was rising and for a moment I felt that the Labu – the name the Moken sea gypsies give to the tsunami – was still close, hovering. In 2008, watching the effects of the cylcone that hit the Burma coastline, and later in March 2011 seeing the images of the tsunami that devasted Fukushima, I was transported back to what happened on the Andaman coast, and reminded of the terrifying power of the earth, wind and water, and of our human fragility in the face of it. But in both cases there was a sense of being distanced, not unmoved but removed from the immediacy of the events that were taking place on the screen. I realise now that having played a minute role in the process of recovery on the Andaman coast, and being in close daily contact with loss, despair, and courage was tranformative. It was partly what impelled me to carry on being involved in humanitarian work. I now live most of the year in Spain where I help those who are dying, and their families, prepare themselves, and I am part of an association teaching professional carers how to integrate spirtual practice into their work.

Writing the stories in *After the Wave* in 2005 was my way of both coming to terms with the suffering as well as expressing the amazement I felt as a witness to the extraordinary human capacity to live through horror and disaster, and to continue. It was my homage to the essence of the humanity that I feel is timeless and universal. When the interview appeared in the Bangkok *Post* one of the quotes chosen came from the story in this collection called 'Closure' in which, through the narrator, I state that I do not believe there is ever any true closure. At least, it is true for me. Ten years after the tsunami I am still processing the events of that Boxing Day, and recognising the link they have to what I am doing and who I am today.